Best W[illegible] Good
Luck

Larry Jacobs

The Frozen Journey

by

Larry Jacobs

authorHOUSE™

1663 Liberty Drive, Suite 200
Bloomington, Indiana 47403
(800) 839-8640
www.AuthorHouse.com

This book is a work of fiction. People, places, events, and situations are the product of the author's imagination. Any resemblance to actual persons, living or dead, or historical events, is purely coincidental.

First published by AuthorHouse 05/24/05

ISBN: 1-4208-4045-2 (sc)

Library of Congress Control Number: 2005903554

Printed in the United States of America
Bloomington, Indiana

This book is printed on acid-free paper.

Chapter 1 THE BLAZING SUN

January 8, 2050, areas in the world that are normally quite cold are now registering very high temperatures. This exists throughout the world. One such area is Gate City, South Dakota, which registered an all time record temperature of 102 degrees on this winter day, January 8, 2050.

Day after day the heat continues setting records throughout the world. Everyone is wondering why this freak weather is occurring. Two Gate City men are puzzling over this strange condition. They are Bill Morton and George Rich who work at the city's nuclear power plant. They live only a short distance from the plant, and they talk as they walk home together.

Bill said, "Boy, if it's this hot in the middle of the winter, I hate to think what it'll be in the middle of the summertime. Why, it will flat boil our brains out."

That's sure the truth," replied George. There were millions of people in the country asking why the sun was blazing down day after day, week after week, with no end in sight.

While most people were just wondering about the strange conditions in the world, some men were trying to find the answer as they peered toward the sun with their powerful telescopes. One such scientist, H. L. Harelson, stayed around the clock at the Mount Palomar telescope site. People in many communities, some hotter than Gate City, were dying on the sidewalks and streets by the thousands.

The blazing inferno continues on, unabated, while the scientists work feverishly on the problem. Harelson asked for a news conference to be held in three days.

On the day before the planned conference, the northern town of Gate City, with a population of 200,000 had a temperature of 110 degrees at 8:00 a.m. Finally the day for the conference arrived. It was held on the outskirts of Houston, Texas in a historic old building with blue walls and ceilings and hardwood floors.

The conference was attended by newsmen from all over the world, as well as scientists from various fields. The main speaker was to be Harelson, who was introduced by scientist, Jack Burlson. Fifty-seven year old Harelson was a short, heavyset man, bald, with a beard and bold brown eyes. He had been in astronomy for thirty years and was well respected in his field. The air was charged with excitement as he started to speak. The air conditioners labored to cool the 125-degree outside temperature.

Harelson started his talk by saying that telescopes on the ground were not able to get a true story of what was happening on the sun. He said that the only solution would be to send a series of rockets to orbit the sun. He proposed that these rockets would carry cameras to take pictures of the sun and computers to analyze nuclear reactions of the interior of the sun, sunstorms, flares, and other phenomenon, which might tell the facts as to why the sun had turned into such a blazing inferno.

Harelson went on to say that he hoped that one very real fear he had would not prove to be true. This was the fact that the sun might be getting ready to nova after getting hotter and bigger until it engulfed the planets of Mercury and Venus. This was what is called the red giant stage. Harelson felt that is as far as the sun would expand, the heat problem would not be the only problem. When the sun reached its furthest out expansion, it would also be very bright, some estimates have put it at 10,000 times brighter than normal. To give contrast, Pluto, which is the furthest out planet in our solar system, receives 1/2500th the heat and light the Earth does. It would be so hot that it would dry up all the Earth's oceans, seas, lakes, and rivers and would burn out its atmosphere. Some estimates have put it if the sun reached Venus, it would be 2,600 degrees Fahrenheit. Life would then cease to exist on Earth.

Harelson said that if this fear were realized, the sun would collapse into itself, becoming a white dwarf. During this collapse, the nova explosion would first occur since by then the sun had used up all available hydrogen. For the sun to exist it has to convert hydrogen to helium. Because of the fact that the entire weight of the sun is collapsing onto itself, this causes enormous pressure and when this mass hit the helium ash core it caused an outburst called the helium flash. If the Earth itself has survived up to this point it will survive no longer because it would be incinerated. In fact, all of the planets in our solar system, clear out to Mars, would be destroyed by this horrible helium flash. So how would Neptune and Pluto fair out of this? A lot better than Earth because they are so far from the sun they would survive, but would be badly burned. After that the sun would eventually become a white dwarf star much smaller than Earth. The sun's matter would become very dense, weighing into the hundreds or maybe even thousands of tons per square inch. There are millions of the burned-out stars.

Harelson fervently hoped that this catastrophic chain of events was not occurring on Earth, but his scientific mind told him that it was a real possibility.

Astronomer Harelson said, "Now, I don't want to cause a panic, as I am not 100% sure that what I fear is happening, but it is a possibility. I want to assure all of you here in this room, as well as people all over the world, that we do not know what the trouble is, and we won't know for sure until we send spaceships to find out. I will tell you, though, that right at this very moment a ship is being readied to send on this mission.

"Our present day rockets can obtain speeds of up to 1,000 miles a second or 3,600,000 miles an hour. The sun is 93,000,000 miles away, so we should have some information about 25 hours after launch."

Harelson concluded his talk and opened up the floor to questions from the newsmen. A reporter asked how many spaceships would be sent up. Harelson answered three. The next newsman asked how long after the ships reached the area of the sun would information be received back on Earth. Harelson said that it would take about three days to analyze the information after it is received. Another question was whether the rockets would be manned. Harelson said that they would not be manned. The final question asked how close the ships would come to the sun and would they stay in orbit around the sun. The audience was told that the spaceships would be a million miles from the surface of the sun and they would stay in orbit around the sun to continue sending back information for weeks. With this final question and answer, the meeting adjourned.

The day following the news conference, the temperature reached 116 degrees at 10:00 a.m. in Gate City, South Dakota. The next two days registered 120 and 125 degrees.

On March 18, George Rich and Bill Morton were on their coffee break at the nuclear plant in Gate City.

George said, "It's at this time of year that we often had blizzards with two feet or more of snow on the ground and winds of 60 miles per hour or more. I just can't believe it."

"Boy, I can't either," replied Bill. "There is quite a history of blizzards and cold weather here in March, so this freaky weather is quite a contrast, that's for sure."

The coffee break and conversation on weather ended and the two men went back to their work.

On the next day in Gate City at 1:30 p.m. the temperature reached 128 degrees Fahrenheit. As the next few days passed temperatures all over the world soared. It reached 134 degrees in

Gate City. Most businesses were closed and the town was at a virtual standstill. A person could only work out in the sun for an hour or so at a time. Therefore the workdays averaged about four or five hours a day for a three or four day week. Television news bulletins urged anyone who did not have essential work to do to stay indoors.

The heat was causing the north and south polar caps to melt, which resulted in severe coastal flooding with a great loss of life and property damage in the billions of dollars.

The information being received at scientific laboratories revealed the scientists' worst fears were true. The sun had grown slightly bigger, which confirmed that the sun was indeed going to explode. It could happen tomorrow, a year, ten years, or even a hundred years from now, but it was sure to happen.

The terrible nightmare was true. The Earth and solar system were doomed.

Chapter II THE PREPARATION

Now the Earth is doomed. The survival plan that finally evolved is to mass-produce spaceships like automobiles, by the millions, then move the Earth's population to the star Proxima Centauri.

Proxima Centauri was just a little over four light years or twenty-five trillion miles from Earth. The nearest star to Earth, not counting our own sun. Even though the rockets could travel at tremendous speeds of up to a thousand miles a second, it still takes 792 years to travel there from Earth. Mans' average life expectancy is 100 years and women could expect to average five years more.

Scientists discovered a way to transport living persons to distant stars by encasing their bodies in coffin-like boxes and freezing their bodies to a minus 273 degrees centigrade. At this temperature the bodies are in suspended animation and will not deteriorate. It would not matter whether it took hundreds, thousands, or even millions of years to reach a star, as the people could be frozen during all or part of the trip. At the end of the journey they could be thawed out and ready to start a new life.

Before this critical time, there had already been cases of freezing people and then thawing them successfully. There were many failures also. The people who had been frozen were those who had died of an incurable disease. When a cure had been found for the disease, they were thawed, treated, and brought back to life. The longest that anyone had stayed frozen before this time was twenty-five years. Theoretically then it should be possible to freeze people for the required 792 years and then bring them back to life. But, as the system had not been 100% successful, there would be some risk in the venture. However, there was no other known way to even attempt to make the long journey to Proxima Centauri, so it would be necessary to take the chance.

The most luxurious spaceships for the trip would be a lot longer and wider than any used before. There is quite a contrast from the first manned rocket to the moon on July 20, 1969 and the luxurious spaceships of today. The spaceships to make the voyage to Proxima Centauri were 1,000 feet in diameter, saucer-shaped, and three times longer, containing barbershops and movie theaters. Because the spaceships would spin, creating artificial gravity, it would be possible to have a swimming pool. Some spaceships are over 2,000 feet long. Each spaceship had its own plan for reaching the star, causing the ships to have a difference in sizes.

When the commander became too old, the children and after them the grandchildren would take over the operation of the ship until they reached Proxima Centauri. Those who died on the voyage would be buried out in space. Board approval is required before couples could have children. The board kept population under control, which was necessary, even though the spaceship was enormous. The United States had 25,000 spaceships.

There are 200 factories producing spaceships in this country. The foreman estimated each factory could produce one spaceship per day if they worked 24 hours a day, seven days a week, because of the emergency situation. On April 1 the temperature in Gate City held at 135 to 138 degrees.

Five thousand people died in Gate City since the terrible heat started. The toll was even worse in other areas. Gate City received news of the melting polar caps that caused more deaths from flooding in the coastal areas. The oceans are moving inland.

There are thousands of suicides. Radio and television newscasts tried to induce calm. About a month later, in May, in the apartment of George Rich, George and his friend, Bill Morton, were trying to keep cool despite the 140 degree outside temperature.

George said, “Well, it looks like it won’t be long until mankind will be taking that first voyage to a star.”

“Yeah, that’s right,” replied Bill. “Have you ever wondered what it’s going to be like at Proxima Centauri?”

“Yes,” said George, “but to me the big question is what if they don’t find life on any of the planets there?”

"They'll just refreeze and head for the next nearest star."

"I hope they find a livable planet around Proxima Centauri, because I'll hate to be frozen for a number of more years," said George.

"I agree with you," said Bill.

"There are definitely planets revolving around the star," said George, "because of the way the star wobbles."

Said Bill, "I hope if there are beings there, we won't get into a war with them. How will they receive us?"

"The only way we're going to know the answer is to finally arrive there," said George.

"That might be sooner than you think. I hear they have increased production of spaceships from 200 to 250 per day."

"I feel sure," said Bill, "not everyone will die. We will survive this holocaust and carry on to some other planet, whether it's in Proxima Centauri's star system or in some other system."

"I feel the same way," George said.

Now, in mid-June and for the past several days, the temperature has stabilized between 144 and 146 degrees. The number of spaceships produced for the flight from Earth had doubled from the 25,000, which had been produced before March. The official count for American ships was 50,062 as of June 15. Other countries were also producing spaceships at an astronomical rate.

On July 4, Gate City hit a record high temperature of 150 degrees. The streets were deserted, as the sun beat down unmercifully and reflected with a blinding light from the buildings, windows, and streets.

People stayed in their air-conditioned homes and apartments, listening to continuous radio and television newscasts. At last, the fearful news came that the sun had grown out and enveloped the space vehicles, which were in orbit around it. The sun has now doubled in size at a much faster rate than the scientists predicted. It is essential the launching of the spaceships begin immediately.

Chapter III THE TAKE-OFF

On July 5, 2050, the first wave of spaceships prepared to take off from Earth with six minutes left before liftoff. On this first day there were to be 250 ships launched. One of this group was the nuclear powered Triton. The Triton was of the modern fusion nuclear powered ships. The last fission nuclear powered spaceship was made 10 years ago. The fusion powered spaceships were faster, more efficient and safer than the old fission spaceships. There were still some fission-powered spaceships around, but almost nobody rode in them anymore, except for some elderly. The Captain and commander of the Triton was Captain Dick York. His crew consisted

1st Officer Russell Simpson, Navigator Jack Harrison, Cook Sam Johnson, Doctor George Benson, and Nurse Susan Sacks.

There are 25 passengers on the U.S.S. Triton, including Scott Jackson, a 35 year old bachelor; 33 year old Sally Sites, a widow; Mr. and Mrs. Bob Swenson and their children, ten year old Billy and eight year old Susie; Carey Norton, John Sampson, Betty Bridges, Mr. and Mrs. George Hanks, Mr. and Mrs. Bill Carlson, George Rich, Bill Morton, Mr. and Mrs. Sam Mickelson, Mr. and Mrs. Bert Taylor, Mr. and Mrs. Henry Fisher, Mr. and Mrs. Gene Tyson, and Mr. and Mrs. Jack Bills.

The food supply for the passengers and crew of the U.S.S. Triton would come from a garden aboard the ship. Sam Johnson is the cook for preparing all the meals for the persons onboard the U.S.S. Triton and he would also tend the garden.

The garden would be composed of a gravel pit with pipes leading into it to supply the needed minerals and water. Artificial sunlight would be provided. Drinking water would be provided by the passengers and crew's own urine, which would be taken through a machine for purification.

Electricity for lighting and for running the onboard computers would be furnished by nuclear engines that also powered the spaceship.

It was 5 minutes before launch. The U.S.S. Triton was to be the first spaceship to be launched, the rest to follow at 6-minute intervals. The U.S.S. Triton was painted red, white, and blue, with U.S.S. Triton in black letters alongside of the ship. The spaceship was 1000 feet in diameter and weighed 30,000 tons.

When the Triton was ten years beyond the planet Pluto on its long journey, all of the passengers would be frozen and remain so until the ship comes to within a year from Proxima Centauri. The machines, which froze them, will then reverse the procedure and thaw them out.

A little different freezing procedure will be used for Captain York and his crew. They will be frozen and thawed at different intervals so they can check out the onboard equipment to make sure it works. At the times they are thawed out, they will also check to make sure that the ship is on course for Proxima Centauri.

It was now four minutes and counting to launch. The passengers had tears in their eyes; and some expressing ideas this is the last time we will see the planet Earth, "We know it's impossible to stay."

As a twenty-year veteran of spaceship command, Captain York's thoughts were of the progress made since that first manned moon landing 81 years ago.

The 21st century humans had landed on Mars and set up a colony on that planet. They had also landed and set up colonies on the planet Pluto and the moons of Jupiter, Saturn, Uranus, and Neptune. Humans had not gone past Pluto because of the tremendous distance between that planet and the nearest star, Proxima Centauri.

July 5, 2050 would be another historic date in the annals of time—that first blast-off to a star outside the solar system. There was three minutes to go and the passengers were readying themselves for the take-off by strapping themselves into the special couches, which would reduce the G-forces on blastoff.

"Please Captain, stop the countdown. I am having trouble with my belt," said George Rich.

"How did you get the belt so twisted?" asks York. "Release the buckle release. I can see that this belt is useless, we will have to get another one from storage."

York installs a different belt for George. "Okay, is everyone strapped in and ready to go?"

"No, sir. I am having trouble with my belt too," said Bill Morton.

"Why, your belt is just as twisted," said York. "I can see that it is just as useless."

Finally the countdown gets started again with just 10 seconds left. Everyone onboard was counting, 9-8-7-6-5-4-3-2-1, blastoff. There was a mighty surge and an earthshaking roar.

The U.S.S. Triton went faster and faster with each second. The passengers and crew were pressed into their couches. It felt like a giant was pressing on their chests. It seemed to be no time at all until the ship had reached its maximum speed of 1,000 miles a second. One minute into the flight, the Earth appeared as a globe, getting rapidly smaller to view.

Chapter IV STATION PLUTO

The Triton, now two minutes into its flight from Earth, was halfway to the moon.

The schedule for Triton as it zipped through space would be:

Moon ------------------------------4 minutes
Mars -------------------------------- 15 hours
Jupiter --------------------- 4 days, 15 hours
Saturn ---------------------- 9 days, 6 hours
Uranus--------------------------------19 days
Neptune ------------------------------31 days
Pluto ----------------------- 41 days, 9 hours
Proxima Centauri ---------------- 792 years

Now, at twenty-four hours into the mission, the U.S.S. Triton was 86,400,000 miles from Earth. The passengers and crew, looking out the spaceship windows, could see their former home, just a pinpoint of light.

The passengers and crew, on the first night of real sleep, spent the night in their luxurious apartments. The crews' apartments being separated from the passengers.

The Captain had made plans for a party to help everyone get acquainted. The celebration started with dinner prepared from produce from cook, Sam Johnson's, garden—corn on the cob, string beans, beautiful red tomatoes, cucumbers, and fresh rhubarb pie.

Captain York said, "This is the most delicious corn on the cob I have ever eaten. You must really have a green thumb!"

After dinner the group adjourned to the big ballroom, where most of them danced until early morning. The most enthusiastic were Scott Jackson and Sally Sites. Sally was very attractive, especially in the eyes of red-haired Scott, who was a very nice looking 6 foot 2 and topped Sally by ten inches.

After dancing for some time to mid-Twentieth Century rock and roll music, Scott and Sally sat on the sidelines, eager to talk and find out more about each other.

"Where are you from?" asked Scott.

"New York City. Where are you from?" she asked.

"I lived in Allentown, Pennsylvania. I was an accountant for an industrial firm," Scott said.

Sally said that she had been a secretary for an automobile agency in New York. As the evening wore on, they became quite well acquainted, as did many others at the party.

Before they retired to their apartments, Scott and Sally arranged to go to a movie the following evening. There was only one theater onboard, and the movie being shown was "Bank Shot", starring George C. Scott.

The party broke up and everyone agreed it had been a wonderful idea.

The next evening at 8:00, Scott was at Sally's door to pick her up and stroll to the movie. They stopped in the lobby of the theater to buy soft drinks and popcorn. Soon after they were seated George Rich and Bill Morton sat down in front of them. George and Bill thoroughly enjoyed the show, laughing several times with the audience.

"Guys, would you please be more quiet?" said Scott.

"I'm sorry," said Bill.

As Scott and Sally watched the movie, they also found themselves watching George and Bill.

The couple walked back to Sally's apartment where Scott asked if he could come in for a nightcap, but Sally said she was tired and had a headache.

So Scott, realizing he couldn't change Sally's mind, gave up and walked back to his apartment.

Captain's Log

July 9, 2050: The Triton has now passed Mars and gone safely through the asteroid belt between Mars and Jupiter. We are now 25,000,000 miles from the giant planet, Jupiter, which is truly the giant planet, because even from this distance it appears massive. It is the biggest planet in the solar system and could swallow 1,300 Earths. Even the great red spot could hold 3 Earths. The planet fills the picture window with its gigantic size. We are 425,000,000 miles from Earth, which we left on July 5, 2050.

▪▪

The days passed quickly as the Triton moved farther and farther out into the blackness of space. Captain York was in the ship's library, Scott and Sally were taking a swim, and Cook Johnson was tending his garden. Other passengers were reading or playing basketball in the gym.

Captain York looked up from his reading as 1st Officer, Russell Simpson, came in. "Hello," said York and Russ returned the greeting.

"It's been a long time since we've been on a flight together," said the Captain.

"It sure has been," said Simpson, as each checked the onboard equipment, "I'm mighty glad to be working with you again."

<u>Captain's Log</u>

July 14, 2050: The U.S.S. Triton's space travelers saw Saturn as the ship passed through its orbit. The Triton is now 886,000,000 miles from Earth.

The silence of the ship was broken by the wailing sound of the emergency siren.

"Quick, check the ship's engines!" ordered Captain York.

"Aye, aye, sir!" said Russ.

"What do you want me to check?" asks Navigator Jack Harrison.

"Check all of the ship's computers," said York, "and I will check out everything else. Then I want us to meet right here when we are all done."

"Aye, aye, sir!" said Russ and Dick.

A short while later and the crewmembers meet at their designated rendezvous point.

"So, what's wrong with the engines?" asks York.

"Nothing, sir," answers Simpson.

"Okay, so what's wrong with the computers?" asks York.

"Nothing, sir. They are working just fine," said Jack.

"Everything I checked was okay too," said York. "So, it's obvious the siren itself is malfunctioning."

"Hey! What do you think you are doing? Don't mess around with the ship's siren!" said York.

"I'm sorry," said George Rich.

"So, why were you touching the siren?" asks York.

"Well sir, I didn't know that it was a siren. I was just curious about it. I just barely touched it and it went off."

"Okay, I don't want you ever to touch that siren again or you will be in big trouble with me!" said York.

"Have we got an understanding?"

"Yes, I understand."

"Good."

Captain's Log

July 24, 2050: The U.S.S. Triton just passed through the orbit of Uranus. We have now gone 1,779,000,000 miles since leaving Earth.

Once again, there is the wailing sound of the ship's siren.

"What do you think, sir? Is it just George fooling around with the siren again?" said Russ.

"This time I don't think it is, after the scolding I gave George the last time," said York.

"Then you seriously think there could be something wrong?" asks Russ.

"Yes, I do," said York.

Later on, the crew checks the whole ship over once again.

"I can't figure it out. I thought for sure this time that there was something wrong with the ship," said York. "I have to think this time there is indeed a malfunctioning siren. Let's go check it out."

"Hey, don't touch that siren!" yells York.

"I'm sorry," said Bill Morton.

"So, why were you messing around with the ship's siren?" asks York.

"Well sir, I thought I saw a hairline fracture, and as I was checking it out, it went off," replied Bill.

"I don't want you or your buddy George to touch any of the ship's equipment or I am putting you in the ship's brig."

"Now Captain, by ship's equipment, what do you mean? Can I use the ship's swimming pool?" asks Bill.

"Of course. You know that is available for anybody aboard the ship."

"How about the gym?" asks Bill.

"Yes! Yes, of course!" said York. "I tell you what I am going to do. I am going to make a list for you and George of the ship's equipment that is off limits to you. If you or George touch anything you are not supposed to, I can assure you that you will go to the ship's brig."

"Okay, I am sorry."

"Good."

Captain's Log

August 6, 2050: The U.S.S. Triton passed through the orbit of Neptune. The temperature outside the ship is minus 300 degrees, but inside the Triton it is a comfortable 72 degrees. The ship is now 2,779,000,000 miles from Earth.

It is late at night and nobody aboard the ship can get to sleep because of the terrible noise. Captain York goes out of his apartment to see what the clatter is. As soon as York gets outside of his apartment, he recognizes the sound; it is hard rock music. He heads down to where the passengers' apartments are located. As he gets to the hallway, he notes passengers out in the hall with scowls on their faces. Captain York knocks on the door of Bill Morton's apartment.

"Hello, Captain," said Bill.

"Turn down the music," said Dick.

"I'm sorry, I can't hear you. Let me turn down the music."

"Okay, keep the music at that level right there," said York. "You are not the only one aboard this ship. You are going to have to be more considerate of other people."

"I'm sorry, sir. It won't happen again."

Captain's Log

August 16, 2050: 41 days have passed since we left Earth. We are now in the vicinity of Pluto, the last planet from the sun in our solar system. We will stop off at Pluto to pick up supplies and to chart and plan our course to Proxima Centauri. We are now slowing down for landing on Pluto. We are 3,650,000,000 miles from Earth.

▪▪▪

As the U.S.S. Triton moved in closer to Pluto the only city on the planet could be seen. The city was encased in a large glass and plastic dome. In just seconds, U.S.S. Triton landed on the surface of Pluto, a short distance from the city. Everyone onboard started putting on their spacesuits so they could venture out into the hostile world of Pluto.

The group is now outside the dome of the city. In order to get into the heart of the city, they had to be transported by the underground transit system, which ran in vacuum tubes, which developed speeds of 1,000 to 1,500 miles per hour.

The Earth group boarded the vacuum trains. The city, Harelson, with a population of 43,560, was named after the astronomer H. L. Harelson.

Not all of the people of Harelson used the transit system. Some chose the nuclear powered cars to drive around the city. In the office of Harelson's Mayor, Virgil Catlin, Captain York visited with his old friend of fifteen years.

York said, "It's sure been a long time since I've seen you. How long have you been the mayor here?"

"It's been about two years," Virgil answered. "How would you like to go out to dinner with me?"

"That would be just great," said York.

Over a delicious steak dinner at one of the plushest restaurants in town, the two old friends had a good visit about old times and about plans for the future.

Virgil Catlin said, "We had plans all set to build another city, but we learned that the sun is about to go nova. Now our plans are to blast off this planet. I've heard that the sun has tripled in size and at some places on Earth the temperature has risen to 185 degrees or more. We're already noticing changes. Our temperature outside the dome has always been about minus 430 degrees Fahrenheit, but it is now up to a minus 399 degrees. True, we've got a long way to go, but eventually there will be no safe place in the solar system, even clear out hear on Pluto."

"I agree," replied Captain York.

After dinner, Virgil took the captain on a tour of the city, then back to the spaceship, where Captain York would have to make plans for the journey on to Proxima Centauri.

Captain York, 1st Officer, Russell Simpson, and Navigator, Jack Harrison started right in on the job of charting the course and take-off from Pluto on their continuation to Proxima Centauri. They worked late before retiring to their rooms for a good night's sleep.

Chapter V LEAVING STATION PLUTO

At this time, we are in a historical first. We have not only escaped Pluto, but we are the first humans to escape the solar system.

"I propose a toast," said Captain York.

The champagne glasses were raised in a tribute to the historical occasion. Proxima Centauri, a southern star in the constellation Centaurus, will truly be a ray of hope for all people of planet Earth.

Several days pass and Pluto appears as a pinpoint of light, and U.S.S. Triton goes deeper and deeper into space. Everyone aboard is happy and contented, especially Sally and Scott.

Captain's Log

July 5, 2051: It has been on year since the voyage began. In that year, the U.S.S. Triton has traveled 29,466,000,000 miles and is 26,889,000,000 miles from Pluto.

"Would you like to go out tonight?" asked Scott as Sally opened the door.

"Yes, I sure would!"

"How about the movies?" Scott asked.

"That sounds great," said Sally.

They started walking and Sally asked, "What's the name of the movie?"

Scott said, "It's a love story called 'Bill and Nancy'."

When they arrived at the theater, the manager, John Simpson, greeted them.

"Well, how are you two?"

"We're just fine," said Scott and Sally in one breath.

"How is the movie?" asked Scott.

"It's good, if you like love stories," answered Simpson.

Scott and Sally walked into the lobby and stopped at the concession stand. Betty Bridges, who ran the stand, asked what they would like.

"Two cokes and two boxes of popcorn."

They walked in and sat down.

"Did you see who just walked in?" asked Sally.

"No."

"George and Bill. Please don't come over and sit by us! Please don't come over and sit by us!" Sally keeps muttering to herself.

Scott and Sally were relieved to see George and Bill sit three rows down from them. During the movie, the couple paid more attention to each other than they did to the movie.

After the movie, Scott escorted Sally back to her apartment. Upon Sally's invitation, Scott came in and Sally asked him if he would like something to drink.

"I'll take a beer if you have one," he said.

After a short time, Scott asked Sally if she would like to marry him.

"I'll promise to be a good husband and treat you like a queen. I'll always love and cherish you. I'll give you anything, at least anything that's in my power to give you."

Sally finally said, "I'd love to be Mrs. Scott Jackson."

"Great," said Scott.

Scott said that he would see Captain York first thing in the morning about performing the ceremony.

When Scott went to see the Captain the following morning, he assured him that he would be very glad to marry them, but that he couldn't allow them to have children while they were on the journey.

Scott said, "I don't understand why we can't have a child. Sally and I want a baby right away."

"The reason I can't allow it, is because there are a number of other couples aboard the ship that want to have children too. This would eventually overburden the ship."

"I will tell Sally, but she will not be happy." Scott then left the Captain to his work and went back to his apartment.

As the days went by, Scott and Sally were busy preparing for their wedding. On the chosen day, the wedding was held in the big hall where dances and other activities were held. Everyone attended the wedding. Sally looked lovely in the long white dress, made especially for the occasion. Scott was dressed in a tuxedo.

They stood in front of Captain York, who performed the traditional marriage ceremony. He asked if anyone believed these two people should not be joined in holy matrimony. If so, they should speak now or forever after hold their peace.

"Hey, there's better seating in the middle," said George Rich loudly.

"No, I think we've got a better view in the front row seats," said Bill Morton loudly.

"Gentlemen, please find a seat and be quiet," said Captain York.

"Ouch! You stepped on my foot!"

"I'm sorry," said Bill.

Captain York waited patiently for Bill and George to get settled before he proceeded, but he found himself glancing out into the audience to see if the men were all right.

"Do you, Scott, take this woman to be your lawfully wedded wife, to have and to hold, from this day forward, through sickness and health, for better or worse, for richer or poorer, till death do you part, so help you God?"

"I do," said Scott.

"And do you, Sally, take this man to be your lawfully wedded husband, to have and to hold, from this day forward, through sickness and health, for better or worse, for richer or poorer, till death do you part, so help you God?"

"I do," said Sally.

"I now pronounce you husband and wife. You may kiss the bride," concluded York.

After the ceremony, there was coffee and cake, as well as dancing which the bridal couple led off. The wedding cake was a beautiful, tall creation, admired by everyone. Shortly Scott and

Sally retired to their apartment where they planned to spend their two-week honeymoon.

It had been almost a month since Scott and Sally were married. Scott made his way to the barbershop where barber, Carey Norton, is cutting Captain York's hair. First Officer, Russell Simpson, Navigator, Jack Harrison, Dr. Benson, and Scott are waiting their turns.

"Have you got room for me?" asks Bill Morton.

"Sure, have a seat," said Carey.

Bill slipped and fell over Dr. Benson's lap.

"My God, man! You spilled your drink all over my new shirt and you have ruined it."

"I'm sorry, Doctor, but it was just a glass of water. I don't think it would've hurt your shirt."

"Well, I sure hope so."

Finally Bill found a seat and sat down. Norton asked York how he would like his hair cut. York said he would like it quite close on the side and back, but he didn't want any off the top. Norton glanced over at Bill to see if he was okay. As Dr. Benson sat in the corner brushing at his shirt, Harrison asked Scott how married life was going.

"Well, so far I have no complaints, but it's only been a month," he said.

"This could be the longest marriage in history," Jack said.

York stepped down from the chair and Dr. Benson took his place.

"Just give me a regular cut, but leave that growth on my face alone," said Dr. Benson. "I am going for a world's record."

Everyone chuckled a little at this remark. In record time, Carey had taken care of all his customers and they went back to their daily routines.

Captain's Log

July 5, 2060: It has been a decade since the Triton left Earth and we have traveled 294,660,000,000 miles. In just 6 weeks it will be time to freeze everyone for the 782 years left in this long voyage.

"It won't be long until we'll have to be frozen for that long journey ahead," said Scott.

"Oh, I hate to think of being frozen like that," said Sally. "It seems so gruesome."

"Yeah, it does," said Scott. "But we have to do it if we expect to reach the star."

"I guess that's true," Sally said. "But maybe one or both of us won't survive the freezing. I don't want to be frozen. I want a baby now. I'm scared."

"I'm scared too."

Tears started to run down Sally's cheeks. Scott hugged Sally and patted her on the back. "We'll make it."

Chapter VI FROZEN

The U.S.S. Triton was now ten years and six weeks from Earth and ten years from Pluto. It was now time to freeze everyone aboard.

The passengers and crew were to be frozen in metal cylinders with clear windows that allow viewing into the cylinders. The temperature will be lowered to –273 degrees Celsius, which is over 400 degrees below zero Fahrenheit. The passengers are to be frozen for 781 years. They will automatically be frozen and then automatically thawed at the journey's end.

The passengers were now in the room in which the freezing would be done. The –273 degree temperature is called absolute zero, as that is the coldest temperature possible. At that temperature, there will be no deterioration whatsoever on the human body, it will last virtually forever.

The first to get into their cylinders are the Swensons. As they lay down inside the cylinder, the door shuts automatically and the freezing process starts.

Other passengers follow the Swensons, slowly at first, then more quickly. The crewmembers, the last to go into their cylinders, are in a different room from the passengers. After the passengers have all been frozen, the crew walks down the hall to their room for freezing.

Captain York, as well as the rest of the crew, is dressed in his uniform with the U.S. flag on the arm. The flag is a replica of the one painted on the side of the Triton. The crew all enter their cylinders at the same time and the doors clang shut. The Triton, with its frozen cargo, continues its trek through the never ending void of space.

Captain's Log

July 5, 2150: It has been 100 years, a lifetime since we started on this journey through space. In the century since we left Earth, we have traveled two trillion, 946 billion, 600 million miles, almost a half of a light year. We have come a long way, but we have a long, long way to go yet.

York and Simpson waste no time as they go right to work checking the computers and other equipment aboard the Triton. After the equipment check is completed, they walk all through the spaceship. They make a stop at the room where the passengers lie frozen in their cylinders. They look into each cylinder to be sure everything is working properly.

York says, "You know, they look just like they are having a restful nap instead of being frozen solid."

"Yes, they do."

A few moments later they come upon a horrible, almost unbelievable sight. They are shocked to see the rotted, grotesque body of Sally Jackson. After over two trillion miles, the Triton had finally suffered its first death. The men discover that the mechanism in Sally's cylinder had prematurely thawed her body. York and Simpson are so deeply shocked that they couldn't speak, but their thoughts go back to these young people, Sally and Scott Jackson, who had loved each other so much. Why did this have to happen?

The two officers finally get control of themselves and go on to check all the other cylinders to be sure they are working properly, so that this terrible thing wouldn't happen again. After they are satisfied that the rest of the cylinders were all right, they couldn't help turning their thoughts again to Sally.

Russ says, "How are we going to tell Scott? He was so much in love with Sally that the news will just about kill him."

"I know. It's going to be rough to tell him such bad news, but someway, somehow, we'll have to do it. I sure dread it though."

They go on checking out the ship and both are hoping and praying that this would be the last tragedy on the ship. After completing their inspection, Dick and Russ go back to their cylinders to be refrozen until the next time.

Captain's Log

July 5, 2175: It has been 125 years since we left Earth. In that time we have traveled 3 trillion, 628 billion, 950 million miles, a little over a half of a light year.

As he checks the ship's systems, Captain York thinks about several firsts in space that have accumulated on this momentous journey. Among these firsts is the fact that this is the first ship with humans aboard to head for a star and it is the first spaceship to use the freezing process in order to reach its goal, so many miles away. York wondered since we have already had our first fatality on the last checkout, will we be able to go on from here with a 100% successful record.

"We can only hope and pray for the rest of us, the journey will be successful and mankind will be able to start again in a new solar system," he says out loud.

Right away, he went to the passengers' room to the cylinders and checked them to reassure himself that there indeed had not been another tragedy. He found them to be all working properly. He then checked the rest of the ship to find everything else was working properly. Then he went to his cylinder to be frozen again.

Chapter VII
TROUBLE?

Captain's Log

July 5, 2200: One hundred and fifty years have gone by since this nuclear-powered spacecraft left Earth. We have traveled 4 trillion, 419 billion, 900 million miles in this century and a half. A little over 2/3 of a light year.

▪▪

Before Captain York and 1st Officer Simpson start on their inspection of the computers and other equipment on the ship, they go immediately to the room where the passengers lay frozen. They want to assure themselves that there has not been another tragedy such as the one that befell Sally Jackson two inspections ago. They find, upon making a thorough inspection, that everything seems to be all right with the passengers.

The two men then go on to continue their inspection of the ship and its equipment. The ship is maintaining its constant speed of 1,000 miles a second.

Suddenly, unexplainably the Triton was speeding up to 1,200 miles a second, then dropping to 975-950, and then back up to 1,000. York and Simpson look at each other in amazement.

“What the hell is happening?” says Captain York; “This is the strangest thing that has ever happened in all of my years of spaceship commanding.”

“I’ll have to agree with you there.”

The ship then starts to pitch and yaw from side to side. York and Simpson look out the Triton’s windows and witness the strangest sight they have ever seen. A strange red glow surrounds the entire ship.

"What do you think it is?" asked Russ, "Do you think the Triton is heating up?"

"I don't know, but we'd better find out right now."

They check the computers and sensors. The Triton was definitely not heating up.

The two men are completely baffled as to what was causing the red glow. The variation in speed and the pitching and yawing continue ever more violently. The lights dim, then grow bright and flicker off and on.

The men continue checking the ship's equipment and find that the computers have gone crazy. They find that all the equipment has gone wild and is undependable. Looks of terror cross their faces and they find they are sweating profusely. They can feel their hearts beating wildly.

The violent gyrations of the Triton continue, and York and Simpson are thrown against the side of the starship like rag dolls. They are knocked unconscious for about thirty minutes. 1st Officer Simpson, the first to regain consciousness, tries to clear his head by shaking it. He realizes then that the terrible shaking of the ship has subsided. Russ starts shaking Dick, who still lay very still.

"Dick, wake up!" Russ shouts, "It's all over."

Dick regains consciousness. "I wish the lights would come back on so we could see what we're doing."

"What do you mean? The lights are on."

"Oh my God, I'm blind, I'm blind," shouts Dick.

Russ looks into Dick's eyes and can tell that he isn't seeing anything.

"We'll just have to thaw Dr. Benson and Nurse Sacks."

The two men, with Dick holding onto Russ for guidance, head for the room. Russ started the machinery that will thaw Benson and Sacks. In a few minutes the doctor and nurse are thawed and come out of their cylinders. Simpson fills them in on what has been happening and asks if they think that Dick's eyesight can be restored.

Dr. Benson says, "Often a hard bump on the head will cause temporary blindness. Usually the sight will return to normal within a few days or weeks. It usually returns spontaneously. If it doesn't correct itself, we'll have to operate. Right now though, I want Dick to go to sick bay and rest completely. Susan and I will give him medication to help him rest and we'll keep a close watch on him."

With Captain York in sick bay, 1st Officer Simpson becomes acting Captain. The situation is hard for Simpson, because he has known York for many years and has become a very good friend. However, now that Simpson is acting Captain, he knows he has a ship to run and he will do it.

The first thing Russ does upon taking command is to check out the computers and other equipment again. He finds everything is back to normal and the ship is sailing serenely through space again. Whatever it was that had caused the trouble, seemed to have passed, but Russ couldn't help wondering if the rough gyrations the Triton had gone through could have thrown them off course. Because he thought he must have an expert opinion on this, Russ goes back to the crew room to thaw out Navigator Jack Harrison.

As soon as Harrison is thawed to his normal condition, Russ clues him in on all that has happened and asks if it is possible that they are off course. Jack answered that it was possible and that he would make a complete check to see where they stand. After two hours of intensive checking, Jack informs Russ that they were definitely off course, but not so far that it can't be corrected.

"That sure is good news. But there is something else, we will have to check whether there has been any damage to the ship."

"What do you think we should take care of first?" asks Jack.

"I definitely think the first priority is to get the ship back on course."

About three hours later, the Triton is back on the proper course and they go to work checking for damage.

After another three and a half hours of checking, Russ and Jack determine that there was no damage to the Triton and they are peacefully on their way to Proxima Centauri.

The next day, Simpson and Harrison go down to sick bay to visit Captain York.

Russ says, "Well, how are they treating you, Dick?"

"Oh, they're treating me pretty good. Was there any damage to the Triton and were we knocked off course?"

"There was no damage, but we were knocked off course. However, we've got that corrected now, so you don't have to worry about a thing," Russ said.

The three men visit a few more minutes before Nurse Sacks comes in and tells Russ and Jack they have to leave so that Dick could get some rest.

"I suppose you've got all those pills for me to take again," says Dick.

"I sure do."

"I'm going to be glad when I don't have to take any more of those pills. You know Susan, I sure hope Dr. Benson is right about believing this blindness will only last two or three weeks. I don't want to lose command of this ship."

"Dr. Benson seems very confident that your blindness will clear up by itself, so I don't think you have to worry."

" I sure hope you're right."

"Okay, why don't you take these pills, lie back, and get some rest. I'll come back and check on you in another hour or so." Two weeks have passed and Dr. Benson is checking Dick over. Dr. Benson scratches his head, as he talks to York in his booming voice.

"You seem to be coming along all right, Dick, and you should be out of here before long."

"I hope you're right. Everything looks black as pitch to me yet."

"Well, don't worry. The thing you need most right now is just rest and relaxation. I know it's hard to do, but it's necessary if you want to get back to normal."

As Dr. Benson is leaving Dick's room, there is a knock on the door and in walk Russ and Jack, who visit Dick everyday.

"Come on in fellows," says Captain York. "How's everything going?"

"Just fine," Russ and Jack answer together.

Dick shouts, "Hey, Russ, I'm starting to see shadowy shapes of you guys!"

"Say, that's great," said Russ.

Dick's sight returns rapidly and within five minutes he can see everything in the room as clearly as anyone.

"I can see! I can see! Quick, get Dr. Benson."

Russ and Jack run out of the room and return with Dr. Benson, whose face is covered with a tremendous smile.

"You were right," says Dick. "It took just the length of time you predicted to regain my sight. I want to thank you and Susan for the wonderful care you've given me."

"I'm just mighty glad to see you back to your old self again," says Benson.

"Well, I guess this means I can get back to the job of running this ship again."

"Just a minute. I think you'd better stay here another week so that we can be sure that you won't have a relapse."

"But, Doc, I feel just fine and I can see perfectly."

"I know, Dick, but we don't want to lose it all now."

"All right, you're the boss."

After expressing their happiness for Dick, Jack and Russ go back to their work.

Chapter VIII WHO IS FOLLOWING THE TRITON?

Captain's Log

July 5, 2250: The U.S.S. Triton, two centuries into interstellar space, has traveled 5,893,200,000,000 miles in 200 years, almost 1 light year. First Officer Russ Simpson and Navigator Jack Harrison are helping me to make our regular checkouts.

York, Simpson, and Harrison have been thawed out to make their regular checks of the Triton. They complete checking on the frozen passengers and then go on to check out the crew, including Dr. Benson and Nurse Sacks, who had been refrozen after making sure that Captain York had recovered completely from his accident during the checkout fifty years ago.

The men also checked on the ship's recorders and computers to make sure another incident like the one that happened fifty years ago didn't happen again. After determining that everything on board is all right, the three men sit down for a little visit before being frozen again.

"What do you suppose caused the wild antics of the Triton?" asks Russ.

"I'm just making a wild guess, and I may be way off, but I wonder if we didn't come near a black hole," answers Dick. "I think we were far enough away that we weren't sucked in, but close enough to cause the Triton to act so erratically, but I feel that this is something that will never be definitely answered."

Adds Jack, "I'm sure it's something we will never know for sure."

As the men end their visiting and are heading back to the room to be frozen, Captain York glances out the window and exclaims, "Hey fellows, look out there!"

The other two men join York at the window and are amazed to see three strange craft sailing alongside the Triton. One is cigar-shaped, one is saucer-shaped, and the third is a wing-type craft. At first they stay some distance from the Triton, and then start to move closer. Soon the three men can see windows in the sides of the mysterious ships, but cannot see who or what is controlling them.

Suddenly, the saucer-shaped craft turns a blood red, then yellow, then green, and starts flashing and pulsating. The craft goes to the front of Triton followed a short time later by the winged and cigar-shaped crafts. Then the saucer falls back alongside the Triton while the other two craft take up positions along the other side. The winged craft falls further back until it is behind the Triton. They surround the Triton in this position for several hours. Suddenly, the three alien vessels zip out ahead of the Earth spaceship.

"What do you make of that, Dick?" asks Jack.

"I don't know, but it must be beings from another star system."

"Do you think they mean any harm?" asks Russ.

"I don't know," said York. "I sure hope not, because we're unarmed."

As the men watch, the three craft continue their antics, staying near the Triton throughout the day and night. The three men decide to take shifts to watch the strange ships, which continue the next day in formation around Triton. The saucer-shape is out ahead, with the cigar-shape on one side and the winged craft on the other. They stay in this formation without variation throughout the second day and night. It seems that they don't mean any harm to the Triton or its precious cargo. If they had meant harm, it seems reasonable that they would have done something before this length of time. It seems that they are more curious about the Triton than anything. The three men watching from the Earth ship hope that if it is just curiosity, that's the way it will stay. The question goes through their minds. What do they want?

The third day of this strange vigil dawns, and Captain York comes to relieve Jack on watch. York asks Jack if anything has happened during his watch.

"Nothing has happened and they've maintained their formation."

"Well, you'd better get some sleep. I'll take over now."

"Don't hesitate to call me if something should come up," says Jack, as he walks back to this room to get some rest.

About an hour into York's watch the saucer ship starts circling the Triton. It continues this circling for about twenty minutes, then goes back into formation with the other craft. They continue in formation for about an hour and a half. Suddenly, the saucer craft starts changing colors, yellow, green, blue, and a blood red, before vanishing from sight.

York blinks in amazement. A few minutes later, the saucer reappears as suddenly as it had vanished. York thinks for a minute that the reason that the ship seemed to vanish was that it probably developed such tremendous speed that it was out of sight in the blink of an eye. If this were true, it would make the speed of the Triton appear as nothing in comparison.

Shortly, the other two strange craft disappear in the same way as the saucer had earlier. They then return and assume the formation again. They continue in formation until it is time for Russ to take over the watch. Just as Russ arrives at his post, the three spaceships take off again at tremendous speed, leaving the Triton behind as if it were standing still.

"Did you see that?" York asked.

"I sure did."

"I wonder what they use for a propulsion system?"

"I hope if they come back that they're not warships planning to wage war with us when we are unarmed."

"I don't think they mean us any harm. If they did, I'm sure they would have shown it by now."

"I think you're right."

The spacecraft did not return during Russ's 8-hour shift, nor did they return the next day or the day after that. Captain York decides to discontinue the watch and the three men go back to their chamber to be refrozen.

Chapter IX TRANSITION

Captain's Log

July 5, 2350: The U.S.S. Triton has been flying in interstellar space for three centuries now, and in that time, we have traveled 8 trillion, 839 billion, 800 million miles, almost 1 ½ light years.

Captain York, 1st Officer Simpson, and Navigator Harrison have awakened from another frozen sleep and in about an hour and a half, they have checked all the equipment, including the ship's recorders and computers. They make sure that there was no one following them or that they did not run into another bad area in space again, that might have thrown them off course. But instead, they found everything a-okay, the ship is still maintaining its thousand miles a second speed.

"Say, why don't we swim for awhile before we go back to be refrozen," says York.

The others agreed and they spend a couple of hours in the pool, York and Simpson racing each other, followed by Jack practicing diving. When they get out of the pool and are on their way back to the freezing room, they continue talking about the strange craft they had witnessed on their last checkout of the ship. Russ again wondered where the alien craft were from.

York says, "I don't know where they came from, but I'm sure glad they're gone." They agree and go into their cylinders to be frozen again

Captain's Log

July 5, 2450: Starship Triton has traveled in interstellar space four centuries. In that time it has traveled 11,786,400,000,000 miles, almost 2 light years.

Captain York was the only person thawed for this checkout of Triton. It took him about 2 ½ hours to complete his duties and as he headed back to his cylinder to be refrozen, he decided to check on the passengers. As he looks into the cylinders, all of the passengers seem to be resting peacefully. Suddenly, he sees George Rich coming out of his cylinder. He can't believe it. As he walks over to George's cylinder, George disappears. York looks inside his cylinder to find George lying like normal.

York walks to the other side of the room and sits down. A short while later and Bill Morton looks like he is coming out of his cylinder. York goes over and investigates to find Bill still in his cylinder.

"What's happening? Am I going crazy? Should I thaw out Dr. Benson and Nurse Sacks? Has the freezing indeed taken a toll on my brain? What should I do?

"Maybe the light and shadow of the room is making me think this is happening. In reality I'm just imagining it. Before I thaw out the doctor and nurse, I think I'll just sit down here and wait awhile."

An hour goes by and nothing more happens. "Am I alright? After all, it's been a long time since the last hallucination. I really don't like seeing the doctor if I can help it. I know from experience that I always feel very nervous and uncomfortable in their presence. I think I'm okay. I'm going back to my cylinder."

Captain's Log

July 5, 2550: For 500 years, Starship U.S.S. Triton and all the men and women aboard have been traveling through interstellar space. During this time, Triton has gone the tremendous distance of 14 trillion, 703 billion miles, almost 2½ light years from Earth.

Helping on this checkout of the Triton is 1st Officer Russell Simpson. It took an hour and a half to do a complete check of the ship, which included the passenger compartment. They find everything okay, so they head back to their cylinders. They talk as they go.

"I should tell you that I had quite an experience on the last check-out."

"How's that, sir?"

"Well, I started hallucinating."

"What do you mean, sir? What happened?"

"I saw George Rich and Bill Morton come out of their cylinders. Of course, in reality it really didn't happen. I was just seeing things."

"Are you alright, sir?"

"I believe I am."

"You feel fine now, but you could continue with flashbacks. Do you want to thaw out Dr. Benson and Nurse Sacks?"

"No, I don't think that will be necessary."

"I'm worried about you, sir."

York paused for a minute, "Okay, maybe it wouldn't hurt to have a quick checkup."

A short while later and Dr. Benson and Nurse Sacks are thawed out and filled in on what was happening.

"Okay, Captain, I want you to go down to sick bay for a complete physical examination."

The first test that Dr. Benson and Nurse Sacks performed was on Captain York's brain. After that the entire body.

"Well, how did I come out?"

"You passed with flying colors and you are free to go."

"But why did I have the hallucinations in the first place?"

"After all, you are a starship commander and that's a lot of stress. The freezing itself would cause a lot of stress."

"So, that's all it was?"

"That's right. I'll be surprised though if we don't have a case of brain damage from the freezing," said Dr. Benson.

"Thanks, Doc. I'm going back to my cylinder."

"Just a minute, I want to say one more thing. Could you see that your 1st Officer takes up more of the load?"

"Yes, I can do that."

Captain's Log

July 5, 2650: 600 years have passed since Triton left Earth. We are nearly ¾ of the way to Proxima Centauri and have traveled 17,679,600,000,000 miles, almost 3 light years into interstellar space.

York, Simpson, and Harrison are thawed out for the check routine. They find everything onboard in perfect working order and are about to go back for refreezing, when York spots an object out in space apparently heading right for Triton. At first it seems to be a very small ball.

"What do you make of that?" asks Russ.

"Well, I have no idea."

The object appears to be on a collision course with the starship. However, after a short time, the men can see that it will not hit them. Instead, it comes alongside Triton, but some distance away. They could easily see now that it is a comet, the long flowing tail clearly visible. Brilliant yellows, greens, and blues radiate from the head of the comet; a beautiful sight to see.

Jack asks Dick if he has ever before seen a comet in space. Dick says that he hasn't and the other two men indicate that they haven't either. They are able to see the comet a few more minutes before it grows smaller and disappears into space.

"I'm sure glad it didn't fly any closer to us, as it could have pulled us off course. Comets are very dense and could have caused quite a pull on the ship if it had come too close."

"Well, I guess we can thank our lucky stars," said Dick.

"Amen," added Russ.

Jack checks to make doubly sure that they haven't been thrown off course. He found that they hadn't so they go to their cylinders, talking about the comet as they walk.

Captain's Log

July 5, 2750: The starship U.S.S. Triton has now gone 20 trillion, 626 billion, 200 million miles through space in the long 700 years since leaving Earth.

Captain York and First Officer Simpson have been thawed for this checkout and as they are running the checks, Russ says, "Well, we're over 80% of the way to Proxima Centauri, so, I guess you could say we're almost there.

They go on with their exacting work. They are all done except for the computer checks. When they get to the last computer, they find that it isn't working. Russ goes around to the back and removes the back cover. Dick holds a flashlight so that Russ can see through the maze of wires and intricate parts. After searching for about ten minutes, he finds a wire, which has apparently juggled loose. He reconnects the wire and the computer starts working normally again.

Dick says, "I'm sure glad it wasn't anything seriously wrong with that computer, as we could have been in real trouble."

After finding everything else in good shape, the two men go back to their cylinders.

Chapter X THE SEARCH FOR LIFE

The Starship Triton is now only one year from the star Proxima Centauri, and the thawing process for all of the men and women aboard is about to begin. The first to be thawed are the crewmembers. Immediately after, the first passenger, barber Carey Norton, comes out of his cylinder after having been frozen 781 years. The crewmembers go down to the passenger section. Norton is shaking his head and trying to adjust himself to normal life after all the years of being frozen.

York says, “How do you feel, Carey?”

“I feel alright. I just want to get my head cleared.”

The crew and Carey then go to look over the rest of the passengers, who are still frozen. However, they are due to be thawed any minute. The crew talks with Carey for a few minutes and then goes back to the job of running the ship.

After checking the equipment, the crew look out the window to see the star, Proxima Centauri, looming ahead. The instruments detect fifteen planets orbiting Proxima Centauri.

The crew and Carey are together as they discover what would be to them a new solar system and a new sun.

“What do you think the chances are of finding one of these fifteen planets to be life supporting?” asks Carey.

“I think the chances are very good,” says Captain York.

“I sure hope so,” Dr. Benson adds.

The men are busily talking and speculating about what they would find on the planets when suddenly, Carey starts hysterically shouting as he brushes at his body.

“There are bugs all over me! Look at them! They’re crawling all over me!”

"What's the matter with Carey? There are no insects on him," says York.

"There are!" yells Carey. He changes to crying that men with blowtorches were after him. Dr. Benson orders the men to get Carey to sick bay immediately.

This was the second tragedy aboard Triton, which reminds York that he has a tough job ahead of him in telling Scott the bad news. He really dreads facing Scott when he comes out of his cylinder.

The cracking of Carey's brain bothers York. He wonders if the freezing could have damaged other brains as it had Carey Norton's. York goes down to the passengers' room where he sees Scott Jackson coming out of his cylinder.

"I wonder when Sally will be coming out?" says Scott.

"I need to talk to you in my quarters right away."

"Why? Is Sally alright?" asks Scott.

"Come on in and I'll tell you all about it."

When the two men are seated in York's room, York says, "I'm sorry to have to tell you this, Scott, but there has been a terrible accident. Sally's dead."

"How?"

York tells him about the malfunction. With tears running down his cheeks, Scott says he would like to go to his apartment for a while. "I understand. If there is anything I can do, let me know."

For several days after receiving the tragic news of his wife's death, Scott stays in his apartment, coming out only rarely.

All of the passengers and crew are now thawed and out of their cylinders. They are living on food pills until Sam gets his garden into shape and harvested.

Captain York has been quite concerned for Scott and has tried numerous times and ways to cheer him, but to no avail. However, York is determined not to give up.

"I know this has been a terrible tragedy for you, but you must live and try to overcome your grief."

"I'm sorry, Captain, but I just can't live without Sally."

York reluctantly leaves, trying to think of a new way to approach him. The next day, when York goes back to Scott's apartment, there is no answer to his knock. He calls to Scott, but still there is no answer.

Finally, York forces the door open. Scott is lying on the floor. He rushes to him, but is unable to get any response from him. He tries to find a heartbeat, but there is none. An empty pill bottle lies next to Scott's body. He summons Dr. Benson, who pronounces Scott dead.

"What's that piece of paper on the floor?" Dr. Benson picks it up and starts to read the note, "I'm sorry Captain, that I was not able to stay with you. But I had to join Sally in heaven."

"I feel very bad about this," said York, "Was I at fault? Could I have done more?"

"Sir, I don't think you were at fault. I think Scott was determined to do this."

Days and weeks go by as Triton continues on toward Proxima Centauri. It takes everyone onboard some time to get over the recent tragedies, but eventually, things get back to normal. They are now off the food pills, as Sam Johnson is again supplying them with his delicious, wholesome garden produce.

The passengers and crew are enjoying a meal, the likes of which they haven't had since leaving Earth. Among the delicious foods from Sam's garden are tomatoes, cucumbers, pears, corn and potatoes. They have delicious wine to accompany their meal.

As they are about to leave the table, Sam says, "Just a minute, there's dessert."

"What is it?" asks York.

Sam brings in the delightful carrot pies he had made. This is the perfect climax to the wonderful meal. When they have all finished, they go their separate ways, York to the ship's library for some reading, some to the movies and others just to take after-dinner naps or walk around the ship.

The weeks and months pass pleasantly as Triton finally reaches the new solar system. York has plotted a course that would bypass the five cold outer planets, which weren't hospitable for life. As he guides the ship toward the inner planets, Triton has achieved yet another first. It is the first time humans have escaped the Earth's solar system and reached another solar system.

It has taken the Starship U.S.S. Triton 792 years to reach the nearest star, over four light years or 25,000,000,000,000 miles from their home planet. In order to accomplish this distance the Triton averaged a thousand miles a second all the way.

Days pass as Triton overcomes the distance of the five outer planets and draws closer to the outermost inner planet, which now appears as a globe to the passengers. Everyone is wondering: Will we find a planet where we can live or maybe even alien life forms?

Captain gives the order to reduce Triton's speed. In a matter of hours, the fusion-powered starship reaches the planet's thick cloud cover. They pass through the clouds and find themselves over a vast ocean. York maneuvers the ship over the water, searching for a land mass on which to land. However, after making a complete circuit of the planet, he found that it is covered with water, three to four miles deep all over the planet. York is forced to order departure from this watery planet. Triton's powerful engines soon carry the ship back into space at 1,000 miles a second, where the search will continue for a hospitable planet.

Simpson and York talk as the watery planet shrinks from view and Triton heads for the next planet. They agree that it was the most watery planet ever encountered. Russ wonders aloud what they would run into on the next planet.

"Let's hope we find life, or at least livable conditions on the next planet," answers Dick.

"I've got my fingers crossed."

"I've got my fingers and toes crossed."

After several days, Triton again slows down for entry into a planet's environment, this time on the second inner planet encountered. The crew all breathe easier as they find themselves over land. They slowly come in for a landing. Triton is touching the surface, accompanied with a loud crunching noise.

"What was that sound?" asks Russ.

"I don't know, but we'll soon find out," says Dick, as the ship shudders and settles several feet into the surface.

Looking out the ship's windows, Dick, Russ, and Jack see what looks like trillions of insects, most apparently dead. The planet's surface is covered with layers of insect bodies, hundreds of feet deep. The only live insects are engaged in deadly battle, as their only food is obtained from eating each other.

Betty Bridges shudders as she looks out at the unbelievable scene, "Let's get away from these horrible bugs. They make my skin crawl."

The other passengers share this opinion. However, before the ship can blast off, they see millions of insects rushing toward them. Dick, Jack, and Russ quickly throw the switches to start the engines. With a thunderous roar, Triton takes off. They level off at about two miles above the surface and begin to cruise across the planet's surface. It is plain to see that the entire planet is covered by the insects that Triton had encountered upon landing.

York gives the order for full power. Soon Triton is back in space at its normal speed of a thousand miles a second.

Suddenly a voice crackles over the intercom; "Captain York, can I please have permission to come aboard the bridge?" asks Bill Morton.

"Yes. Okay, what can I do for you, Bill?"

"Well, sir, I wonder if we haven't missed a golden opportunity by staying on the bug planet?"

"What would that golden opportunity be?"

"Well, Captain, look at the great food supply we would be missing."

"I sure will take that into consideration, but I think I am going to check the other planets out first. If we don't find anything better on the other planets, we'll sure come back to the bug planet."

"Okay, I was just trying to be helpful."

Triton sails on through the blackness and soon approaches the next planet, and once again they slow down for landing. Triton would enter the planet's atmosphere momentarily.

Chapter XI CAPTURED

Starship U.S.S. Triton has landed on the third planet, and all aboard disembark and are walking on the surface. The area is a meadow with a little creek running through it. The atmosphere is almost exactly like that they had known on Earth. It is a warm sunny day with no clouds in the sky, except for a lone, little, purple cloud. This is the first sunlight the people of Triton have seen since leaving the Earth, 792 years ago. Everyone is smiling and happy as they explore the planet.

"Well, we finally made it, after trillions of miles and hundreds of years," says Russ.

"Yes, isn't it great?" answers Dick.

"Did you see that little stream running through the meadow?"

"I sure did."

"Isn't it tremendous? We've finally found a livable planet."

Russ sticks out his hand to shake with Dick and pats him on the back in congratulations.

"I would like to offer my congratulations too," said Jack, as he shakes hands with Dick and Russ.

Soon everyone from the Triton is laughing, shaking hands, and offering congratulations to whoever happens to be near. Two more purple clouds join the cloud that had first been seen when landing on the planet.

"Do you suppose we're going to see our first rain?" asks Jack.

"I don't know. It could be," says Captain York.

Another cloud appears a short distance away from the other three. All of the sudden, the last cloud zips over and joins the others. Then more and more clouds come together and form a circle. The crew and passengers become fascinated watching them. The purple clouds move closer to the Earth people, hovering a few hundred feet above them. They stay like that for about five minutes, then drop to the ground surrounding everyone in a purple mist, with the circle of clouds in a perimeter around them. The clouds start to move in closer.

"I can't breath," shouts Dick.

Everyone is choking and gasping. Soon people are falling to the ground, their bodies twitching. After a short time, the twitching stops and there is total silence. The victims seem to be paralyzed, but they are aware of what is going on around them. The little purple clouds sail across the horizon and disappear from sight.

After about thirty minutes of lying on the ground paralyzed, Captain York feels himself being dragged across the ground. Soon, all the crew and passengers too, are being dragged over the ground but are powerless to do anything about it. They are dragged over to an alien spaceship, up the steps, and into the ship. When they are all inside, the ship takes off with a whirring noise.

Captain York and the other Earthlings then get a look at their captors, giants of nine or ten feet in height. They will learn later that these giants are a race of beings known as Aldans, and they call the planet Draeon. The leader, Zorax, stood ten feet, three inches in height. The tallest Aldan on the planet was Borith, who stood thirteen feet, four inches. They all had high, dome-shaped foreheads, yellow eyes, two holes for a nose, and a slit of a mouth. They seemed to talk among themselves with a humming sound. The Aldans were far advanced over the Earth civilization, especially in psychic powers.

The Aldans' spaceship is three times faster than the Triton. It runs by the magnetic field of planets, through a motor onboard the ship, reversing the magnetism. This is an antimagnetic spaceship, which is far from the fastest of their ships. Such ships were used as shuttlecraft to go from planet to planet in their own solar system.

When they traveled to other stars, they used their Photon propulsion ships that could reach the speed of light. These took photon particles from their sun into the ship, since these particles were traveling through space at the speed of light. This made the spacecraft go at the same speed, 186,000 miles per second or approximately 670,000,000 miles per hour.

The Aldans were by far advanced from Earth in another way. They had discovered a way to live forever through rejuvenation machines. When Aldans grew old and close to death, they would go into these machines, which would completely revitalize all of their organs, tissues, and bones, making them like new again. They were like they had been reborn when they came out of the machine. They could live about 200 years between rejuvenations, so they could live forever, if they continued to be reborn in the machine about every 200 years.

The Aldan spaceship soon landed, after skimming over the planet Draeon. They started carrying the Earth prisoners out of the spaceship and across the ground. They had not left the planet Draeon, but had just landed in another area of the planet. The Aldans soon came to a group of steel cages. They put Captain York and First Officer Simpson in one cage. The rest of the Earth people were put in other cages. There were other beings and creatures in numerous cages.

Next to the cage holding Dick and Russ, was a cage with a creature having characteristics of both human and gorilla. It had buttocks like a man, but fur like an animal. Its face was rather humanlike, but its hands and arms resembled a gorilla's. The cage adjacent to this held a creature with a cowlike body with four legs, but no tail, a big head with a long nose that came to a sharp point, similar to, but not exactly like, a shark's head. The body was white with orange spots. Next to this cage was one containing an almost human figure, except for the long curling horns coming out the sides of its head.

After a couple of hours, Dick and Russ had regained their ability to move.

"I never expected to be a prisoner in a steel cage when we reached Proxima Centauri," said Dick.

"It never entered my mind either."

"I sure wish we could figure some way out of this prison."

"So do I, but I don't see how we could. These bars must be at least two inches thick."

"I guess all we can do is hope and pray that we find some way of escape."

"We'll still have to contend with these giants," answered Russ.

Their conversation stopped abruptly, when the ten foot, three inch frame of Zorax loomed over their cage.

"I am Zorax, leader of a race called Aldans on the planet Draeon. How are you Earth creatures doing?" His telepathic voice sounded deep and gruff in their heads.

"We're doing lousy and we want out of this prison you've got us in," said York.

"You will have to remain here because you complete my collection," said Zorax.

"Where are the rest of my people?" asked Dick.

"They're in various other cages just like yours," said Zorax, who then turned and walked away.

"Come back here, you monster! Let us out of here!" shouted Dick.

Zorax continued walking away without responding. Several hours had passed when Dick and Russ saw two Aldans walking toward their cage. When they arrived at the cage, one of the Aldans opened the door, while the other guarded the entrance. They had brought two bowls, which they now set on the floor of the cage. They told Dick and Russ that this was their lunch and to eat heartily. As the Aldans left the cage, they closed and locked the door, and with hideous laughs said, "Enjoy your delicious lunch now, Earth creatures."

The food in the bowls was a purple color and gave off a strange glow.

"It might be poison," said Russ.

"I guess that's the chance we're going to have to take."

The two men sniffed the strange mixture, but there was no smell to it.

They finally decided to try it. "This is really garbage. It tastes like stale cardboard," said Russ. As Russ and Dick ate, a great number of Aldans and their children walked by the cage. Many of them stopped to look at the two Earthlings. Dick and Russ kept on eating as the Aldans gazed at them with their ugly yellow eyes. After they had finished eating the terrible Aldan food, a large crowd was massed in front of their cage.

A short time after eating, the two Earthlings started to feel strange. Russ started at Dick, "I think you must be the most stupid commander of a starship I have ever seen."

"What the hell has gotten into you?" said Dick.

"It's you that's gotten into me, you dirty, no good rat."

The argument continued until it broke out into a fistfight, with Dick first slugging Russ right on the nose. Then Russ punched Dick in the stomach, and as Dick folded over, Russ punched him again, on the jaw. Then Dick countered with a blow to the mouth that sent Russ reeling into the bars of the cage.

The Aldans watched silently as the fight continued. Dick was on top of Russ, hitting his first officer repeatedly. Russ put his feet against Dick and pushed, sending Dick spinning against the bars, where he hit his head. Dick shook his head as Russ got back on his feet. Dick landed a blow on Russ's chin, which knocked him unconscious. Then, Dick too, fell to the ground, unconscious.

When they regained consciousness, sometime later, neither could remember a thing about the fight, nor even about anything that had happened for several hours before that.

"Well, I know I'm sore all over, and my jaw really hurts, but I don't know why," says Russ.

"I feel the same way."

Several hours after the fight, as Dick and Russ are trying to remember what had happened, an Aldan walks toward their cage with their supper. The crowd, which had watched the fight, had left. As the Aldan reaches the cage, Dick notices that the cage door is open and quietly indicates this to Russ. They rush toward the entrance, just as the Aldan sets the bowls on the ground. However, even though the Aldan is over nine feet tall, he moves with the speed of lightning. He grabs Dick and Russ and throws them back into the cage. Dick gets up and tries again, but he is again thrown back. Russ aims a punch into the stomach of the giant. He might as well have hit a brick wall, for all the Aldan noticed. The strike hurts Russ's hand much more than it hurt the Aldan. The giant Aldan picks up both men, and throwing them to the ground, leaves the cage, locking the door behind him.

Dick and Russ get up from the ground and dust themselves off. Dick walks over to the food bowls, and picking one up, he throws it against the bars of the cage, spilling the glowing, sticky mess down the bars.

"I'm not going to eat anymore of this crap."

"I'm with you on that."

Just then the half-gorilla, half-man beast in the next cage started wailing mournfully. Dick and Russ had heard these cries before during their stay in the cage, but it still unnerves them. As the creature looks into the Earthmen's cage, his lonely, wailing cries turn to a whimper. Dick and Russ move closer, but still stay at a safe distance so that the beast can't grab them with his powerful hands. When they get closer, they see a terrible sadness and loneliness in his eyes, and soon they see big tears starting down his cheeks.

"I wonder why he's so sad," said Dick.

"Do you suppose it is because he's in captivity, or because he misses his mate?" asks Russ.

"I guess we'll never know for sure," answers Dick. "I'd say that he misses his mate most of all."

The beast puts his hand out as if in friendship, but the men thought they'd better not chance taking his hand into their own. The beast soon withdraws his hand, goes over to the other side of his cage, and lies down. There are no more outcries, but he lies facing Dick and Russ, staring at them intently. Soon, he grows sleepy and in a few minutes is fast asleep.

The hours passed and it soon becomes night on the planet, but because of the four moons, which were in the full stage, it was not very dark.

As the night wears on, Dick sees a figure approaching their cage. He nudges Russ. They think the approaching figure is probably an Aldan child, as it is much smaller than the Aldans who had come to their cage earlier. As it draws nearer, they see that it is a female, but probably not an Aldan.

Chapter XII THE RESCUE

The woman comes close to Russ's and Dick's cage, stops, and stares at the two men.

"Who are you, and what do you want?" asks Dick.

"I am Atheasis from the planet Aon, which is the next planet from Draeon. I have come to rescue you Earthlings."

Her eyes turn pure white and beams of light and heat emanate from them. The heat is so intense that Dick and Russ reel from it. They are amazed as the beams from Atheasis's eyes melt the bars of their cage as if they were chocolate candies.

As soon as several of the cage bars are melted, Atheasis says, "Hurry up. We must get out of here quickly, before an Aldan finds you out of your cage. My spaceship awaits you."

"What about the rest of the humans?" asks Dick.

"Later, no time now," replies Atheasis curtly.

Dick and Russ offer no argument. As they enter the spaceship, they see two more women wearing white flowing robes like the one Atheasis wears. They are so absolutely beautiful, their faces and bodies so flawless and perfect, that they make the most beautiful Earth woman appear ugly in comparison.

The women go right to work, throwing switches and preparing for an immediate departure from Draeon. The spaceship is of a photon-drive type, which gains the speeds of light as it streaks through space. Dick and Russ, looking out the spaceship window, see that the planet Draeon appears, now, as a small globe.

The Aon people are very religious, peaceful, and nonviolent. They do not believe in war. They have all the advancements of the Aldans—Photon-drive starships, mindreading, clairvoyance, and rejuvenating machines, with which they could live forever. The one thing they do not have that the Aldans did, was a great store of weapons. They have very few weapons because, of course, they believe in love, tenderness, and affection, rather than in war and violence.

Captain York says, "Atheasis, I have a couple of questions I'd like to ask."

"Yes, what are they?"

"How did you happen to come to our rescue and how do you know our language, like the Aldans did?"

"We rescued you because we wouldn't want to leave anyone to the mercy of the warlike Aldans. We know all about your language, customs, and everything else about you, as we have visited your planet many times. We've observed your planet since the time you were all in caves. We have beams from our starships that allow us to see into your industrial buildings and homes."

"Were your people in the ships that we spotted far out from Earth?" he asked.

"Yes, we observed you and knew long ago that you were coming to Proxima Centauri."

"I guess we should introduce ourselves and become acquainted," says Dick. He introduces himself and Russ.

Atheasis introduces her crew, Barthena and Trais.

"We are sure glad to meet such beautiful ladies," says Dick.

"Well thank you. When we arrive at our planet, we'll take you to our city, Voris, and to the Queen's palace. The Queen, who happens to be my sister, is called Virena and is the Queen of all Aons."

Dick and Russ both express their eagerness to meet Virena. It isn't long until they arrive at the Aon planet. In what seems only a few minutes since they left Draeon, they land just a short distance from the city of Voris. The Aon women, along with Dick and Russ, walk into the city. It is quite a sight to the two men with its mile-high spiral buildings and temples.

"I hope you like our Queen," says Atheasis. "She has been our Queen for five rejuvenations."

"I'm sure we will," say Dick and Russ.

"How long would that be?" asks Dick.

"Well, a rejuvenation is good for 200 years. When we go into the machines, it completely revitalizes our organs, tissues, and bones. Without the machines, our life span would be only about 200 years. We have these machines throughout the city of Voris and all over the planet."

The group soon arrives at the palace and goes inside. As they enter, they see Queen Virena in her white robe, sitting on the royal throne. Atheasis brings Dick and Russ before her Majesty and introduces them.

The queen smiles at them, "Welcome to our planet, Captain York and 1st Officer Simpson. You are welcome to stay on our planet as long as you wish, as we have plenty of room."

"I surely appreciate your hospitality, but I wonder if I could make a request of you?" says Dick.

"What is it?" "Would it be possible to rescue the rest of my crew and the passengers of our ship?"

"They have already been rescued," answers Virena.

"Would you like to see them?"

"Would we ever! Where are they?"

"They are in various rooms here in the palace. I'll have Atheasis summon them."

A few minutes later, Atheasis returns with the passengers and the rest of the crew. There is unbelievable joy on the faces of all of them.

"But where are Carey, George, and Bill?"

"They were killed by the Aldans," says Dr. Benson.

"Oh, no."

The group is soon laughing and talking among themselves when Queen Virena asks if they would like a tour of the palace. The Earth people think this would be a wonderful idea, so they proceed on the tour, where they finally see some of the Aon men. They, like the Aon women, are probably the most handsome in the galaxy or even in the universe, and they too wear white flowing robes.

As the group goes through the various rooms they notice that they are all painted blue, just like the big room in the spaceship that brought them here. They come to a room, which is empty except for a metal cabinet with a window in the door at a height which would show only a person's face if they were to enter the cabinet.

Is that a rejuvenation machine?" asks Dick.

Trais, their guide, says yes. Dick asks if they could look it over. Trais assures them that they are welcome to look into it, and she opens the door of the cabinet. When the Earth people look into the cabinet's interior, they see that it is also of metal construction on the inside, and has many dials, switches, and gauges. After the group has inspected the machine and proceeded through the rest of the palace, it is time for the evening meal. In one of the large rooms, a long table has been set to accommodate all the Earth people as well as Queen Virena and her court.

"Well, I imagine I had better acquaint you Earth people with our Aon food," says Queen Virena.

She points to a platter with a vegetable about the size of an average pumpkin, but black in color. A few slices, showing the dark blue interior, had been cut from it and were lying on the platter.

"This is called frais. This is called jaron," pointing to a bowl containing what appears to be peas, but white in color. "The long, stringy, orange-colored food in another bowl is called veriff. The green beverage in the pitcher is called tiken."

The Earth people find that the Aon food tastes like nothing they had ever eaten before, but the consensus is that it is delicious. Queen Virena sits at one end of the long table with Atheasis at the other end, but when Virena requests food at Atheasis's end of the table, Atheasis sends the dish to the other end with her mind control only. It comes to a perfect landing at Queen Virena's elbow. Mind control is just another of the great powers possessed by the Aons, which is a source of great amazement to the Earthlings.

"We have had these powers for the past ten rejuvenations," says Barthena.

"I'm very sorry," says Virena, "but we've forgotten that you require sleep, which we don't. We know that it is customary for you to sleep in beds, so we have workmen constructing these now, so that they'll be ready when you wish to retire."

"Well, we surely appreciate that," says Dick. "Your hospitality is fantastic.

"I would like to ask you a question, if it wouldn't be too personal. Why were your ships at the area 200 years out from Earth."

"No problem," says Atheasis. "We were just doing some studies and research on your sun's red giant stage. When your ship was 200 years from your home planet, Earth, that was when the helium flash occurred."

"Then Earth has already been vaporized," says Captain York.

"That is correct, Captain. Your home planet is now gone."

"Oh my God, no," says Betty Bridges as a tear runs down her cheek. "Those poor people."

There was a moment of silence at the table as all of the Earth people try to take all of this in. Everyone at the table has a note of sadness on their faces.

Finally, York says, "Well, we all knew that was going to happen. If there was anybody left on Earth, nobody was going to survive the red giant stage of the sun, let alone the horrible helium flash, for that put an end to Earth itself."

"Well, I can tell you that the Earth star was a spectacular sight in our skies over Aon," replies Virena.

"Oh, please tell us what it was like for you people here," responds York.

"Okay, before your sun made its last gasp, there were three outbursts. The first one was the brightest, it shone so bright in our Aon skies, that it was as bright as a full moon is to your Earth.

"It stayed that bright for weeks. It was even visible in our daylight skies. Then the Earth sun started to dim down. It got very dim, to the point we could barely see it. Then within a short while after that, there was a second outburst. The Earth star became very bright once again, but not nearly as bright as the first outburst. It stayed very bright for a few days, then dimmed down once again.

"It dimmed down to the point where you could just barely see it. It stayed at this dim level for just a day or two. Then came the third outburst. The Earth's sun became bright once again, but not nearly as bright as the first or second time. It started to get very dim once again. In fact, it got so dim you could no longer see it with the naked eye. It has stayed at this very dim level to this day, never to brighten up again.

"We, of course, all knew that it meant the people of Earth were in really big trouble. But we were perplexed as to just what to do and took it all really sadly. We all saw, in our minds, thousands of ships fleeing Earth, trying desperately to escape this horrible nightmare."

The captain says almost to himself, "So, when the sun got to its brightest point, that was when the dreaded helium flash occurred. And when the sun became so dim that you could no longer see it with the naked eye, that was when the sun had dwindled down to a white dwarf star and cooled off."

"Yes, Captain, you are correct," said Atheasis.

"But what was that area of space 150 years out from Earth, that caused so much havoc to the Triton? Was that a black hole?" asks Captain York.

"No, it wasn't," says Atheasis, "Many eons ago, when we first started interstellar travel, we were under the impression that all of interstellar space was perfect. Now, of course, we know that idea is not true. There are certain areas of time and space where there are flaws in the fabric of space-time. Little ripples, or bumps if you will. We have no trouble with these areas anymore because we have mapped this entire galaxy so we know just where they are and, therefore, know how to avoid them. But, to the inexperienced interstellar traveler, there is real danger."

"That is very interesting and I think I understand what you are saying because Earth scientists had a theory about the universe right after the big bang, that this caused a rippling effect and later on caused a clumping in space that caused the galaxies to cluster in space. From that theory, I got my own idea, this overall rippling and clumping effect also caused the universe to knot-up. In certain areas, you would have these really bad knots in space. And we came too close to one of these knots 150 years out from Earth. Is this assessment accurate?"

"Yes, Captain. In fact, we saw, in our minds, thousands of ships being destroyed in this area. We saw just a few ships escape the area, and they were thrown off course by it. Out of those few that were thrown off course, only one got back on course to Proxima Centauri."

"You mean to tell me that we were the only one out of thousands launched from Earth, to make it here?" Captain York asks.

"That's correct."

"Would it be possible, out of the ones besides us that were thrown off course, that they never made it to any other stars?" asks Dr. Benson.

"Yes, that is possible, because since then we have not gotten any more readings from our minds," says Trais.

All of the Aons nod in agreement.

"Do you people realize what this means?" asks Dr. Benson.

"What?" replies York.

"This means you are a super hero, Captain," says Dr. Benson.

"Now wait a minute, Doc. I'm not that great of a hero. We wouldn't have made it here without your great medical staff, and we wouldn't have made it here without the excellent navigating from Jack or from my 1st Officer. So, it wasn't only I that got us here."

"Well, all we can say is because you are the Earthlings to make it here, you are very special people to us," said Atheasis.

"I'm happy to hear that," said York. When dinner was over, Captain York said, "I think I'll take a walk to work off the meal. Would anyone else like to go along?"

Although most of the guests decided to stay where they were, Dr. Benson, Jack Harrison, and Russell Simpson decide to accompany Dick. They walk along, looking into the different shops and buildings. It seems to them that about every other building is a religious temple.

Jack says, "It is sure good to see you guys again."

"I'm certainly glad to see you, too," says Dick, "and I'm sure glad the Aons rescued us."

"I was wondering if we'd ever get out of there alive," says Dr. Benson.

"Well, that was certainly going through our minds, too," says Russ.

As they continue their walk, the Earthmen notice an old man coming toward them. This is the first old person they have seen since arriving at the city of Voris. As the old man draws nearer, they see the wrinkles in his face. He looks just like people on Earth when they grew old. The old man stops at a rejuvenation machine, in front of one of the buildings. He steps into the machine and shuts the door. They can see his face in the window of the cabinet.

As he turns on the switches of the machine, they see red, yellow, and orange lights flashing inside the cabinet. They stop to watch, and soon, there is a whirring noise that lasts about a half-hour, followed by a screeching sound.

The lights continue to flash, while the strange sounds are going on, and continue even after the sound stopped. Then the lights go out and the man opens the door and steps out, a young handsome man, like the other Aons they have seen on this planet. The man turns and walks jauntily away from the group of Earthlings, who start back toward the palace.

When they arrive back at the palace, they see only Trais, Barthena, and Atheasis.

"Where is everyone?" asks Dick.

Atheasis answers, "some have gone to their rooms, and others to one of our temples for meditation."

"I believe I'll go to my room and lie down for a while as that walk kind of tired me out," says Dr. Benson.

Dick, Russ, and Jack are left alone with the Aon women. Trais asks if the men would like to go with them to the regular meeting of the Aons in the morning.

"I would," says Dick, "I don't know about the rest of our group."

The other two men indicate that they would like to attend the meeting and after a short time, they all retire to their rooms for the night.

The next morning, it turns out that all the people of the Triton had decided to go to the Aon meeting. After breakfast they head for the temple where the meeting is to be held. Everyone is down in various pews with Dick, Russ, Jack, Atheasis, Barthena, and Trais all in the same pew.

The meeting begins with an Aon minister giving a sermon about the most Supreme Being in the universe, Zith, who had landed on the Aon planet over 7 ½ rejuvenations ago.

"We must never let ourselves forget the teachings of Zith. Before Zith came, we were just as warlike as the Aldans, but He taught us that violence is evil and horrible. He told us that the only way to live is with love, tenderness, affection, and gentleness. Love is good—war and violence are evil.

"If it wasn't for Zith, we would have not progressed and have the good life that we have now."

After the sermon, the natives sing Aon hymns and offer prayers to Zith. The meeting is over and everyone leaves the temple.

The next day, York, Simpson, and Harrison decide to go for an afternoon hike through the forest of Cinan. The Queen had told them about the forest, a short distance from the city. She said that it would be a beautiful walk for them. They reach the edge of the forest and continue down the path, which leads to the other side of the forest. They marvel at the beauty of the scenery. They soon come to an area of needle-like rock formations and cliffs. A little further on, they see a little stream curving through the forest.

"Virena was sure right," says Dick.

The other men nod.

"It sure is hot, though," remarks Russ.

"You're right, Russ," says Jack. "Why don't we rest a little while?"

They decide to rest for a few minutes in a nice little meadow. When the men get up and continue their walk, they come to rolling hills and a valley, about midway in the forest. After about a half-hour they reach a bowl shaped area at the bottom of which is a lovely little lake with sides slanting gradually down to it, making it easy for the men to walk down to it.

As they come closer to the water's edge, they catch sight of some Aon girls swimming in the lake. One of the girls comes out of the water and they see that she is nude. The other girls follow her out of the water and they, too, are nude. Although the men are quite close, the girls are not aware of the men's presence. Although the men are absolutely speechless at their beauty, they decide that they shouldn't embarrass the girls by making their presence known, so they quietly leave and start back to the palace. The girls, laughing and talking as they put on their robes again, have not even noticed the Earthmen.

On the way back to the palace, the men discuss the unbelievable beauty of the girls they had inadvertently seen unclothed; they had never seen anyone of such flawless beauty of both body and face.

As the three emerge from the forest a few minutes later, they suddenly notice hundreds of ships hovering over the Aon capitol. Without warning, the ships send down beams, vaporizing the buildings they hit. They quickly realize the warships came from the planet Draeon.

Chapter XIII THE WAR

All the Earthmen can do is watch from their vantage point at the edge of the forest. They want to rush to the palace to see if their newfound friends are safe, but they know that this would not be wise, as they would only be killed. So, they stand there watching as Zorax and his fleet of warships rain havoc on the city. Finally, the Aldans end the attack and head back to their home planet of Draeon.

The Earthmen head back into Voris, eager to see if their friends are safe. When they reach the city, they see a lot of empty spaces where, just a few short minutes ago there had been structures. The beams from the Aldan warships vaporized every building they touched. When the men reach Queen Virena's palace, they find it miraculously standing untouched. They walk up the steps of the palace and into the big hall leading into Virena's court. There is no one there.

"Let's see if we can find the underground shelters the guide told us about when we toured the palace," says Dick.

They soon find the long stairway, which leads down to the shelters. After a long walk, they come to where her Majesty and her court are huddled in one corner of the big room. After assuring them that the attack is over and the ships gone, York asks, "Is everybody all right?"

"Yes, all of us in the palace are all right," says her Highness, with tears still running down her cheeks, "but, we'd better get out into the city and see if anyone there needs help."

The Queen, her court, and all of the Earthmen and women head upstairs to the main floor of the palace. When they reach the main floor, Queen Virena, Atheasis, Trais, and Barthena start out the back door to where the magnetism craft were parked. These craft, powered by the magnetic field of the planet, are used, not only for travel around the city, but also for shuttling to different planets of their solar system. Out in space, they can reach speeds of 10,000,000 miles per hour. They are very versatile, able to travel at a very fast speed, a very slow speed, or even to hover. However, even at their fastest they cannot compete with the Photon-drive starships which travel at the speed of light. The Aons, like the Aldans, use the Photon-drive spaceships mostly for travel to different stars.

"Would you like us to go along with you? Perhaps we could be of some help," asks Captain York.

"That would be real nice of you."

So Captain York, First Officer Simpson, Navigator Harrison, Dr. Benson, and Nurse Sacks, all go along with the Aons to survey the damage to the city and to pick up anyone who might be injured and helpless. The Earthmen and the Aons fly slowly over the city, stopping from time to time to survey the destruction.

Shortly they spy an injured Aon man. They pull the vehicle alongside him, get out, and walk up to him. They quickly see that his leg is badly damaged, being cut almost in two. Dr. Benson takes charge, saying that they must get the man to a hospital immediately and indicating that the injured man might also have internal injuries.

Benson asks if there is anything that they can use as a stretcher. Her Majesty informs him that a stretcher won't be necessary. She then presses her fingers to her forehead and shuts her eyes. The man levitates and slowly floats through the air and into the craft. Nurse Sacks opens the door of the craft when she sees him rise into the air, and the man floats inside the craft and gently comes to rest on the couch inside the craft.

After delivering the injured man to the palace, where he could be thoroughly examined and treated, they continue the inspection tour through the city. The final tally of casualties is 560 dead, 10 injured, and 20% of the city of Voris destroyed.

When the Earthmen and Aons arrive back at the palace, they find work has started right away to help the injured patients. Some had only minor injuries, and they were treated and released. The badly injured were rushed to operating rooms in the palace, where Aon doctors and nurses attended them with assistance from Dr. Benson and Nurse Sacks.

Queen Virena returns to her room, where Captain York goes to consult with her, as she sits quietly on her throne. York asks what they have in the way of weapons. She informs him that the only weapons they have are three beam cannons, one beam rifle, and one beam pistol.

"That's sure not much with which to face the well-prepared Aldan war machine, but I guess it's better than nothing."

"We've been strongly thinking of disposing of all our weapons."

"That is something you sure can't do now, with that madman on the rampage. Where are these weapons?"

"I will not tell you, nor can I allow anyone else to disobey Zith."

"We can't just sit here and do nothing. Someway, somehow, we've got to stop Zorax, because if we don't, you know you'll become a conquered, defeated people."

"If Zith wishes to be conquered, I guess that's what we will be," says Virena quietly.

Dick feels it would be useless to argue with her anymore, and he leaves in utter frustration. As he heads back to his room, he meets Jack and Russ. They ask Dick how he had come out in his talk with the queen. Dick tells them that he had no luck, but he would like to know where the beam guns were stored.

"We're certainly going to have to do something," says Russ. "Zorax won't stop at just conquering the Aon planet. He'll go on to conquer this whole system and even the whole galaxy."

"That's right," answers Dick. "But what can we do? I've never felt so helpless in all my life."

"I guess we can only hope that the Queen will change her policy," says Russ.

The men then continue on to their rooms. In the meantime Dr. Benson, Nurse Sacks, and all the Aon doctors and nurses are working feverishly on the injured. They continue their efforts all through the night and for several more days. The less seriously injured and the ones who had undergone surgery are kept under medical care, some even for weeks longer.

A couple days later Nurse Sacks, making rounds, comes to a room in which are a little Aon girl, about six years old, and a little boy of about eight. She has pills for the children to take, but before she can give the children the pills, the little girl asks where her parents are. Nurse Sacks says that she doesn't know, but will try to find out.

"Oh yes, please do!" cries the little girl.

"All right, but first I want you to take your pills. Then I will tell you a story."

"That sounds real good," says the little boy.

Nurse Sacks begins the story. When she is about halfway through, she notices that both children have fallen asleep so she quietly leaves the room. She then goes from room to room to check on the other patients and give them medicine, where indicated. As she walks along, she thinks of the little boy and girl. She knows that both parents had died in the Aldan invasion, but she can in no way bring herself to tell them the sad news.

After finishing her rounds, Miss Sacks goes for a night's rest. The following evening, the Earthlings and Aons are at supper, and

Captain York tells Queen Virena what a wonderful meal they are again enjoying. As the group eats and chats, suddenly her Majesty tells them that they must all go quickly to the underground shelters.

"I see a large fleet of Aldan warships heading for Aon right at this moment. The group quickly obeys her command, for what her highness saw in her mind was indeed correct."

This fleet of warships sent by Zorax was far greater than the first one. Shortly after the people are settled in the underground shelters, the fleet of Aldan warships arrives in the Aon atmosphere. There are so many ships that they literally blot out the sun, bringing darkness to the city of Voris.

When the Aldan ships arrive over the Aon capitol, they hover a few hundred feet above the buildings. Then they start sending beams from their ships, vaporizing building after building. This second invasion lasts about two hours, after which the Aldans again take off for Draeon.

When it seems that it is safe to come out of the shelters, the Aons and Earth people again see the destruction caused by the Aldans. By some miracle the palace still stands. Now, half the city lies in ruins. There are more than 600 dead and fifteen injured in this latest attack.

Captain York again goes to see her highness, who again sits on her throne. He tries to convince her to use some kind of defense against the brutal Zorax.

Tears start rolling down Virena's cheeks, "Yes, Captain York, we must devise a defense against Zorax. I cannot let my people suffer anymore."

"I am glad you finally see that we must do something."

"I wonder if the great Zith will forgive me. Or will he bring his wrath down upon me and my people? And what about the Aon citizens, will they condone this?"

"I think you will be forgiven by Zith and by your people. I can't see that you have a choice."

"I will have to take the chance," replies Virena.

"I certainly understand your feelings, but my men and I will handle the weapons and your people will not even have to touch them. Now, let's not waste any more time. Show me where the beam cannons and other weapons are stored."

Virena leads York downstairs to a locked room in the shelter. The cannons are on stands. The cylindrical barrels of the cannons are about six or seven feet long, made of a transparent material, making it possible to see right through them.

Dick says he will get Russ and Jack to help him carry the cannons upstairs. Queen Virena shows Dick a button on the side of the cannon. When this button is pushed, the cannon collapses within itself, becoming very compact.

"When you get the cannon where you want it, just push the button again, and the cannon will return to its original size. When we get back upstairs, I will show you how to operate the guns and cannons."

Dick goes upstairs and gets Russ and Jack, who help with the equipment. When the three cannons are in place in front of the palace, they push the buttons, returning the cannons to their original form and size. The Queen then shows them how to operate the cannons as well as the other weapons.

Two days pass. The Earthmen, as well as the Aons, are becoming very nervous, waiting for the next attack. The Queen informs them that she sees in her mind, the Aldans leaving the planet Draeon with another large fleet of Zorax's warships. The Aons and Earthlings, except for York, Simpson, and Harrison, who are manning the three cannons, all retire to the underground shelters.

The three men scan the skies for sight of the warships. Soon, they spot them approaching the city at tremendous speed.

"Are you guys ready?"

"You bet we are!" answers Russ.

Captain York throws the switches, readying the beam cannons. The Aldan warships are hovering just above the rooftops, getting ready to send down the deadly beams. York aims his cannon and fires at one of the Aldan ships. The bright beam races from the barrel of the cannon, and when it reaches the warship, the ship and the Aldans inside, vanish into thin air. Russ and Jack follow Dick's example and vaporize two more ships.

"Wow!" exclaimed Jack, "These are sure some weapons!"

They all give a cheer at their success in knocking out the Aldan warships.

The three men go back to work trying to destroy as many enemy ships as possible. In a short time, they have vaporized a dozen, but the Aldans soon get wise to what is happening to their brother ships. They put a force field around their ships, thus making the beam cannons useless.

"Let's get down to the shelter," says York.

After the Aldan raid ends and the surviving ships return to Draeon, the Aons and Earthlings come out of the shelters to see how much damage has been done this time. They find three-fourths or seventy-five percent of the city now destroyed, and there are 625 more casualties (620 dead). The Aon doctors and nurses, assisted by Benson and Sacks, are again kept busy for some time, tending the injured. York, Harrison, and Simpson are having a meeting in York's room.

"It sure looks hopeless for the Aons," says Dick.

"Yes," says Jack, "There's no stopping Zorax now."

"You know, what surprises me though, is that the Aldans haven't sent in their armies to occupy the city," says Russ.

"I have been wondering the same thing," replies Dick, "They must surely know what bad shape they left the city in after the second raid."

"Maybe Zorax just enjoys destroying the city," answers Russ.

"I think you may be right," said Dick. "The sadistic monster." Jack concludes, "It seems obvious to me that we won't have long to wait before Zorax does send his troops to take over the city."

Jack and Russ go to their rooms for a night's rest. It isn't long until the three men are sound asleep, as they have had a very busy day.

As the Earth people sleep and dawn approaches, a large fleet of Aldan warships again encircle the city. This time the ships land at the outskirts of Voris. Ships surround the city. The Aldans disembark and start marching through the Capitol City with beam rifles slung over their shoulders and beam pistols strapped around their hips. Ten-foot three-inch Zorax and thirteen-foot four-inch Borith lead the Aldan soldiers. The Aldan soldiers met with very little resistance from the Aons. Most of the Aons just stand in front of the buildings and temples, looking in terror.

Zorax and Borith reach the palace, where three lovely Aon girls are sitting on the steps. With terror in their eyes, the girls run up the steps with the evil Zorax and Borith giving chase. The girls are no match for the lightning speed of the giants. Zorax catches hold of one of the girls, spins her around, and with one sweep of his giant hand, rips off her white gown. A white glow from her eyes sends powerful rays toward Zorax, but he at the same time, sends out beams from his own eyes, which neutralizes the girl's. She then fights, kicking, hitting, slapping and biting, but Zorax overpowers her and rapes her. Borith rapes the second girl.

The screams from the girls bring York, Simpson, and Harrison from their beds to witness the attacks on the women of the Queen's court. They are powerless to help as Borith pulls out his beam pistol when the Earthmen approach them.

"That's far enough," says Borith.

The Earthmen are forced to watch the fiendish attack upon the women, who had proven to be such good friends to the Earth people.

Chapter XIV CAPTURED AGAIN

The Aons are now a conquered and defeated people. Not only has Voris, the capitol city, been conquered and occupied by the Aldan troops, but the other Aon cities all over the planet are under the control of the Aldans.

York and the rest of the Earth people have been taken prisoners and returned to the planet Draeon. When they arrive back at the Draeon planet, they are taken again to the cages where they had been held before. The only ones not returned to the cages are York, Simpson and Harrison, who are to be treated to a special surprise by Zorax. Zorax, with two more giant Aldans, escorts the three Earthmen to a fenced area covering many acres.

As they near this area, Russ says, "Look! There's the Triton!"

Not only was the Triton on display, but there were many other sea, air and land vessels that could have been found on Earth many years ago.

Zorax says, "Go ahead, Earth creatures, and look over my collection! There will be more added to it after I conquer and become master of the galaxy."

"Sure, you did a great job of conquering an almost defenseless people like the Aons. I would like to see how you would do against a really well-prepared foe," says Jack.

"How dare you contradict me! I shall conquer and be master of the galaxy," says Zorax, "Once I have conquered this whole solar system, I will have enough materials and resources to launch large fleets of warships throughout the galaxy. Then the galaxy will be all mine."

"You are a mad man," says York. "I will do everything in my power to stop you."

"You stop me!" shouted Zorax, with a fiendish laugh, "Ha! Ha! You or anyone else cannot stop me."

"I do not want you to call me Earth creature anymore. I am Captain Dick York, Commander of the U.S.S. Triton."

York turns away from Zorax and says to Jack and Russ, "Come on, let's see what they've done to the Triton."

They find that she had not been tampered with. After looking the ship over thoroughly, they proceed to look over the other vehicles in the fenced area. The first display is three marine jet fighters.

"I read an article once, that took place long ago in about the 1950's," says Russ. "It told about three marine jets that gave chase to a UFO and disappeared. These ships sure look like the ones pictured in that article."

"It seems to me that I heard something like that, too," adds York.

The three men continue their tour through the area, looking at the vessels glimmering in the midday sun, some of them merely rusting hulks. They see seafaring Earth vessels such as sailing ships, battleships, destroyers, freighters, oil tankers, and even modern Earth vehicles such as atomic-powered airplanes and cars. When they finish their tour, three Aldan guards escort them back to their cages. They are in the same cage as before, alongside the cage of the part-man, part-gorilla. The other cages also hold the same prisoners as before, including the creature with a shark's head and a cow's body and the horned man.

A few hours after the Earthmen had been put back into their cage, they see an Aldan approaching them. When he reaches their cage, they see that he is carrying their supper, the same purple food as before. The Aldan sets the three bowls of purple food down and leaves.

"Well, here we go again, with the terrible Aldan food," says Captain York. "I'm not going to eat this slop until I get so hungry that I'll be forced to." The other men add their "Amen" to that.

"It looks now like we'll be stuck here for a long time, maybe for the rest of our lives," says Jack.

"It kind of looks that way, since Zorax has this solar system practically in his hands, probably the galaxy, too," says Russ.

"We won't get rescued again by the Aons, that's for sure," says Captain York.

As the Earthmen talk, the half-man, half-gorilla creature starts growling, snarling, and shaking the bars of his cage. As he shakes the bars, the three men notice that he is shaking the whole cage.

"If he keeps that up, I wouldn't be surprised if he escaped," says Russ.

But the creature finally tires of the shaking and growling and goes over to the corner of the cage and lies down. The men soon lie down also, and try to get a little rest. They are awakened by a terrible scream. The gorilla-type animal has bent the bars of his cage enough to escape. When he is out of the cage, he comes upon an Aldan, whom he grabs in a bear-like hug, and shakes him fiercely in his powerful arms. The Aldan is soon as limp as a doll. The Earthmen feel sure that the Aldan is dead, but the gorilla-man picks the Aldan up and throws him into the air; he lands about fifteen feet up into a tree. Yellow Aldan blood starts oozing from his head and he lies lifeless and silent. The gorilla creature then starts to run for freedom, but he doesn't get far as a couple of Aldan men spot him and aim their beam rifles at him. He is vaporized into nothingness.

Several days later, Dick, Russ, and Jack are forced to break down and eat the Aldan food. Although it was as tasteless as it had been before, they don't get the violent reaction from it. They must have become immune to it.

In the mid-afternoon of the next day, York happens to look up into the sky where he sees strange craft. They are neither Aon nor Aldan ships. Shortly after York spots the alien craft, a beam comes from it, striking and vaporizing the Aldan warship. Then a beam from one of the Aldan ships vaporizes an alien ship. The Aldans continue fighting, trading ship for ship, but the alien craft outnumber the Aldans about two to one. The Aldan retreat with some of the alien ships in pursuit. The rest of the alien ships land within sight of York and the other two men. When the aliens come out of their ships, the Earthmen notice quite a contrast between them and the Aldans.

These beings are not more than four or five feet tall and almost as wide as they are tall. Their arms appear very big and powerful. As soon as these short men step out of their ships, they are met by Aldans and a terrible battle ensues, with an exchange of fire from their beam weapons. York notices a hand to hand fight between one of the giants and one of the short aliens. They have both lost their weapons, someway, and are slugging it out with bare fists. At first, the Aldan seems to be beating the alien being unmercifully, but strangely, the little man does not even flinch.

"Will you look at that," says Russ. "That giant isn't hurting that little man one bit."

"It looks like the Aldan is about exhausted from beating him, without doing any damage," says Jack.

"They are sure tough little men," says York.

Finally, the alien being, getting tired of the Aldan beating on him, throws a punch to the Aldan's hip with such force that he flies for about ten feet, landing hard on the ground, some distance away, where he lies motionless.

"Did you see the punch that little man landed on the giant?" asks York.

"I sure did," says Russ.

In a short time, the Aldans break away and start to run for their lives, but a group of the small men give chase. One alien doesn't go after the giants. Instead, he starts toward the cage holding the three Earthmen.

Chapter XV THE MARAANS

When the small man gets close to the cage of the Earthmen, he starts talking to them. He does this without moving his lips, because he does it telepathically. The letters of each word imprint in the Earthmen's minds.

"I am Commander Sashon. I come from the planet Maraan, one of the inner planets of the solar system. When we liberated the Aon capitol, we got a request from the Aon queen to bring Captain York and the rest of the Earthlings back to the Aon planet."

Sashon grabs the cage's bars, bending them wide open, so that the Earthlings can escape. When Dick, Russ, and Jack are free of their cage, they walk to Sashon's waiting spaceship, where they meet the other Maraans inside the ship.

The Maraans are as ugly in appearance as the Aons are beautiful. They have bulging orange eyes, which look about to pop out of their heads. Their skin is grayish, patchy, and puffy. Their noses are broad, and they have only a slit for a mouth. They have not only the two bulging orange eyes in the front of their heads, but also a single orange bulging eye in the back of their heads.

Captain York asks where the rest of his crew and passengers are. Sashon assures him that they are being taken care of, and some of Sashon's men, at that moment, are going to bring them. In a few minutes they are all aboard the Maraan spaceship.

"How were you ever able to defeat Zorax, with his powerful warships?" asks Russ.

"We didn't know ourselves whether we could do it," answers Sashon. "The Aldans had destroyed most of our cities and our capitol was under siege. We thought we were beaten, but we decided that we would fight to the last man, if necessary, in order to stay free of Zorax's tyranny.

"Finally, we broke through and started, slowly but surely, pushing Zorax's forces back. We pushed them all the way to the Aon planet, where we started liberating the Aon cities from the Aldan conquerors. From there our fleet pushed the Aldans all the way back to their home planet."

"It is good to know the war of the solar system is over and that Zorax and the Aldans have been defeated," says York.

"I feel the same way," says Sashon. "Once again the solar system and the galaxy are safe from Zorax."

Sashon now orders his crew to take off from Draeon. The Maraan ship is an anti-magnetic ship, much like the Aon and Aldan ships, but much faster, capable of attaining speeds of 15,000,000 miles an hour, while the top speed of Aon and Aldan ships is 10,000,000 miles an hour. Like the Aons and the Aldans, the Maraans also have photon-drive ships, which can go the speed of light. They also have all the other advancements of the other planets, such as the rejuvenation machines, but they differ in that they are a military power.

About an hour into the flight to Aon, Draeon appears as just a pinpoint of light. Sashon had left men to occupy the planet until the Court of the Worlds could meet and try Zorax and his men for their crimes.

The Earth people are anxious to get back to the Aon planet of beautiful women and handsome men. York is eager to get back to help Queen Virena rebuild her city.

In a matter of hours, the Maraan spaceship lands at the Aon capitol of Voris. Sashon and several other Maraans escort York and the other Earth people to the Queen's palace. The Queen and her people are overjoyed to see York and his people again. The Earthlings are equally pleased to be back on the peaceful planet. The Queen thanks Sashon for his help and says she will be eternally grateful. The Maraans then leave for their home planet.

Queen Virena introduces Tronin, her husband, and their two children, a ten-year old daughter, Serathena, and twelve-year old son Bais. Queen Virena tells York and the Earth people that Tronin had been on a space crusade for six months. They had gone to the two star neighbors nearest to Proxima Centauri. These were only about

1/6 of a light year or 1,209,000,000,000 miles away. These two stars are very close together, only the equivalent distance from Earth to Neptune apart, a yellow star and an orange star. The yellow star has four planets orbiting it. The orange star has no planets. Tronin had spent two months on the third planet from the yellow star, called Terin, which is the only planet of the four that contains life.

The children had gone with their father on this journey. Tronin tells how he felt that they had made real progress in bringing the word of Zith to these very primitive tribal people. He tells how the Terin people were planning when he left the planet, to send four men in a very primitive chemical-powered rocket to the moon that circles their planet at about 620,000 miles distance. Tronin and Queen Virena tell Captain York of their hopes to spread the word of Zith throughout the galaxy.

Captain York volunteers to help the Aons to rebuild their capitol. The Queen tells York that the Earth people are welcome to stay on the Aon planet as long as they wish. She tells him of the fertile land lying to the east of Voris, on which they could raise crops and build settlements. The next city, called Tranis, was fifty miles from Voris. The land her Majesty offers to the Earthlings lies about midway between the two cities.

As the next few weeks pass, the capitol of Voris is coming back to life with the help of the Earth people. Zorax is tried in the Court of the Worlds, and found guilty of war crimes against the solar system of Proxima Centauri.

He is exiled to a remote asteroid, along with his henchmen. They will see no other living people, except when a supply ship or freighter heading for another star stops off to leave food and supplies for the prisoners.

With Captain York, his crew, and the passengers of the U.S.S. Triton settled on the Aon planet, humankind has a new start, with a new sun to provide heat and light. The success of this brave group shows no matter how bad the disaster, people will survive, even if it means leaving their planet and starting on the long, long journey of 25,000,000,000,000 miles and taking 792 years.

Chapter XVI ZORAX ESCAPES

Queen Virena over the years has been quite depressed because of the accidental death of her husband, Tronin. He was coming home 5 years ago from a crusade at the Terin Planet, when the ship's engines malfunctioned, exploding and killing Tronin. It was witnessed by a passing heavy cruiser and reported to Virena. However, she saw in her mind the explosion before it was reported to her. Her children, Serathena and Bais, were married and moved to other solar systems far away and consequently seldom saw them anymore. Virena was slowly getting over her depression.

The year is 2857 Earth time, fifteen years since the Earthlings arrived on the Aon planet. Their colony has increased from the original 28 to the present 86. They have become very good friends with the Aons.

Captain York directs the work in the fields as the Earth people harvest their crop of Aon food. York is actually 854 years old, but he was in a frozen state for all but eleven years of the long trip, so he is the equivalent of a 73-year-old man. He is six-foot-two-inches tall with brown eyes, but his original brown hair has changed to a silver gray. He still wears his old flight overalls and black leather boots, which he keeps as shiny as a mirror.

York looked up from his work to see an Aon woman approaching. "Well, hello there, Atheasis. How are you?" he greets her.

"I'm just fine," said Atheasis. "How would you and the rest of your group like to come to the palace for dinner?"

"I would love to," said York as he turned to ask his co-workers' opinion.

Their answer was, also, in the affirmative, so Atheasis led the way to the big anti-magnetic ship, which would take them to Voris. Atheasis, wearing the usual long, white, flowing robe of the Aons, led the way up the steps and into the ship. Once inside the ship, the Earthlings were met by two even more beautiful Aon women, Trais and Barthena.

"Hello, Earthlings, it's so good to see you again," said the two lovely Aon girls.

"Well, I say it's good to see you ladies again, too," said Captain York.

"It's been a long time since our last visit," said Trais.

"Yes, it has," said York's First Officer, Russell Simpson, "but, we've all been very busy trying to get our crops in."

"I'm sure you have," said Barthena.

"I think we'd better be on our way to the palace," said Captain Atheasis.

With that, the other two Aon women quickly responded, turning on switches that sent the ship on its way to the Aon capitol. Soon they arrived at the city of Voris, and then to the palace. They all disembarked and entered the palace, going directly to Queen Virena's throne room, where they found the queen sitting on her royal chair.

The queen asked the visitors to sit down and asked if they would like refreshments. These were served.

"How have my Earth people been doing lately?" asked Virena.

"Oh, we're doing just fine," answered Captain York.

They talked a short time until dinner was announced. The group then went into the big dining hall, where two long tables were set for dinner. During dinner, when Atheasis requested a dish from the other end of the table, Queen Virena sent it to her with the power of her mind rather than with her hands.

"I will never forget the day that you rescued us from the Aldans," said Navigator Jack Harrison.

"Well, that was the least we could do. If you had stayed on the planet Draeon much longer, your people would probably have been killed by Zorax and his comrades," said Virena. "Before you were even captured by the Aldans, we wanted to help you. It's good that you are all safe on our planet."

"I'm sure I speak for the whole group, when I say we are certainly glad to be here," said York.

The Earthlings and Aons are about ready to push themselves away from the table when Virena cries, "Oh, no! Zorax and his comrades have escaped off the asteroid where they were imprisoned."

"What? I can't believe it," exclaimed York.

"How did they do it?" asks Russ.

"They someway took over the supply ship which was bringing their rations. They made their escape in that ship. The United Worlds space patrols are out searching for them at this very moment," explained Virena.

"I knew it. I knew it. I thought all along that they should have been executed instead of being put into exile on that asteroid," said Dick.

"It chills me to the bone to think that the criminal mind of Zorax is loose once again," said Russ.

"Take heart. Maybe the space patrols will locate them and bring them back to justice," said Jack.

"I certainly hope so," said York.

"All we can do is hope," said Virena just as an official newscast confirmed the horrible nightmare that Virena had seen in her mind.

Chapter XVII SUPER FAST

Several months after the escape of Zorax, the Aons and some of the Earth people meet at an Aon temple. In one of the pews sit Atheasis, Barthena, Trais, Captain York, First Officer Simpson, and Navigator Harrison.

An Aon minister is speaking from the podium, "It was through Zith that we started to make real progress. We are, therefore, very grateful for His teachings." After singing a few hymns, the meeting ended and everybody started filing out of the building.

York caught up with Atheasis and asked, “Have you heard whether the United Worlds Space Patrol has any clues as to where Zorax and his comrades might be?”

“No, we haven’t had any concrete evidence from them, except that they are still searching.”

“I sure hope the patrol finds that monster and brings him back to the asteroid where he belongs,” said York.

“It certainly is terrifying to think that Zorax is still loose, but I have confidence that the patrols will find the culprits and bring them in,” said Atheasis.

“I certainly hope they do,” said York.

It was just a short walk from the temple to the palace, and the Earthlings and Aons spent a quiet, peaceful afternoon there. As evening approached, Atheasis, Trais, and Barthena escorted the Earth people back to their colony.

The search for Zorax went on for several more months, but one day news came to the palace that Zorax and his companions had been located. Warships were sent to bring them in. A few hours later another newscast is received at the palace. The news this time, however, turns out to be very bad. All 25,000 warships which were sent out in the search and expected capture of Zorax, have been destroyed with one shot from a powerful beam gun which Zorax and his men had developed in their months of hiding. The beam gun had been developed in a secret laboratory, the location of which was known only to Zorax and his gang. The terrible disaster was witnessed by a passing freighter that managed, somehow, to stay clear of the battle and escaped to give the report.

Zorax's beam gun is believed to be powerful enough to destroy a whole planet with one shot. No one in the Proxima Centauri solar system has a defense against such a horrible weapon. It appears that the Proxima Centauri system is doomed!

Since the solar system was now so helpless, Queen Virena sent out orders for everyone to start preparing starships for launching out of their solar system, to try to escape Zorax and his mighty war machine.

The next few hours were spent feverishly preparing for the escape from the Aon planet. Zorax, however, bypassed the Aon planet and went right to the Maraan planet to get his revenge on

Commander Sashon, who had defeated him in the last war fifteen years ago.

When Zorax arrived in the vicinity of the Maraan planet, he stationed his warship with the super-powerful beam gun thousands of miles from the planet. He, then, radioed down a message to Sashon demanding the surrender of all his military forces or the destruction of the planet with the beam gun. He gave Sashon what would be equal to twenty-four Earth hours to make his choice— surrender or destruction.

During this time, the Aons and Earth people prepared their ships for departure from the Aon planet. Inside one of the Aon starships is Atheasis, captain and commander of the ship. Her First Officer is Trais, and Barthena is the navigator. There are numerous other Aons, including doctors, nurses, cooks, and of course, Queen Virena. Also on this ship are a number of Earthlings, including Captain York, First Officer Simpson, Navigator Harrison, Dr. Benson, and Nurse Sacks. There are a total of 560 persons aboard this Aon starship, which is saucer-shaped and about a mile in diameter with several levels. The first level contains the engines, storage rooms, computers and other equipment. The second level contains the apartments for the crew and passengers. The top level is for recreation and agriculture. It is a photon propulsion ship, which means that it can go the speed of light, 186,000 miles per second, or approximately 670,000,000 miles an hour.

Countdown was done—10-9-8-7-6-5-4-3-2-1-fire and the ship took off, slowly at first, but soon it was traveling silently and serenely through the darkness of space at the speed of light. The Aon planet soon appeared as only a small globe.

York, Simpson, and Harrison were at the bridge visiting with Captain Atheasis.

"Where will we go to escape Zorax?" asks York.

"We plan to pass through the next galaxy without even looking for a livable planet. We will start looking in the galaxy after that," said Atheasis.

"Even going at the speed of light, it will take thousands of years to reach even the galaxy next to us," said Russ.

"Oh no, it won't take near that long. We have a way to speed the ship up," said Atheasis.

"How do you do that?" asked Russ.

"Well, there are interstellar space gas clouds about nine of your Earth months away, and by taking our ship through them, we will be speeded up tremendously," said Atheasis.

"Wow," exclaimed Jack, "that sounds interesting. I can't wait until we get there."

"Do you mean to tell me that by merely going through these space clouds, we will speed up?" asked York, with surprise.

"No, we have discovered a way to convert the cloud energy to usable power for our ships. The formula we have devised for this, we have kept secret for many years," said Atheasis.

"I'm going to look forward, myself, to our arrival at these clouds," said York.

"It seems to me that our Earth scientists had said something about their believing that there was a lot of energy in the interstellar gas clouds," said Russ.

"It's too bad we didn't know the secret of using this power when we were traveling to your star," said York.

"The distance we had to travel from Earth to Proxima Centauri going at our rocket speed, would have been prohibitive if it hadn't been for the freezing technique we used," said Jack.

Atheasis then gave the Earthlings a little tour of the bridge. When they came to a star map on the wall, York asked, "What are the lines shown going to the various stars?"

"These broken lines here are to solar systems where we have established colonies, and these lines are where we have sent spaceships with the Word of Zith to primitive, uncivilized peoples," said Atheasis.

After the tour, the Earthmen went back to their apartments, leaving Atheasis to her duties as commander of the starship. At twenty-four hours into the flight, the Aon starship is billions of miles past the farthest planet in the Proxima Centauri solar system.

When the Earthmen went down again to the bridge, they found Atheasis, Trais, Barthena and Queen Virena in tears.

"Why are you crying?" asks York.

Queen Virena answered, "We have just learned that Sashon has surrendered to Zorax."

"That surely is bad news," exclaimed York, "I had the greatest respect for the little Maraans. They were mighty brave little men."

"I figured they would be forced to surrender to Zorax," said Russ. "What choice did they have?"

"I thought Sashon would probably say 'Go ahead and blow us up. We would rather die than live under your tyranny'," said Jack.

"I sort of had those thoughts too, but when you put enough fear and pressure on people, they will eventually collapse," said York.

"We just know that we're very sorry that this had to happen," said Atheasis.

"I imagine now with the rich minerals on Maraan, that there will be no stopping Zorax," said Russ. "He will now be able to launch large fleets of warships to achieve his goal of conquering the galaxy."

"Well, he certainly has conquered Proxima Centauri Solar System, but I have my doubts about his conquering the galaxy. He will run into a solar system just as strong or stronger, that will be able to stop him," said York.

"I sure hope so," wished Jack.

"Was it Zorax who wrote that nothing would be too horrible for him to do in order to achieve his goal?" asked Russ.

"Yes, it was," answered Trais.

"My God," exclaimed York, "If I ever get my hands on that beast, I couldn't do enough to him."

"He certainly is some kind of horrible monster, all right," said Russ.

"Zorax has destroyed many of our cities and killed millions of our people, but we still forgive them. We do not hate the people, but only the things they have done," said Barthena.

"That's one thing I will never be able to understand about you Aons," said York, "your ability to forgive."

"We learned long ago that hatred destroys the one hating more than the enemy," said Virena.

Now, nine months after leaving the Aon planet, the ship is in the vicinity of the first interstellar gas cloud and heads into it at the speed of light. As the Aon starship goes through the cloud, it goes up to ten times the speed of light. They then go through the second gas cloud, which raises their speed to 100 times the speed of light. The third cloud raises the speed to 1000 times the speed of light, and when they go through the final cloud they are traveling 1500 times the speed of light or a little over a trillion miles per hour.

Chapter XVIII CRISS-CROSS A GALAXY

A short time after the Aon starship had left the interstellar gas clouds, it is speeding along at 1/6 of a light year an hour.

"I just can't believe that at the 287,000,000 miles a second we are now traveling, that we could criss-cross a solar system in a matter of seconds," said Russ.

"Not only that," said Dick, "our journey from Earth to Proxima Centauri, traveling at 3,600,000 miles an hour took us 792 years. At the speed we're going now, we could have made it in 25 hours."

"It certainly blows my mind," said Jack.

"The thing I really notice most, is how the position of the stars changes in just a few minutes, whereas the same changes took many years on our travel in the Triton," said York.

"I have been figuring out some rather interesting facts," said Russ, "If we were traveling in the Triton and knew the secret of getting power from the clouds, we would have been going more than twice the speed of light."

"Yes, that is interesting," said Dick.

"All I can say is that even in my wildest dreams, I never imagined I would ever go the speed of light, let alone 1500 times that fast," said Jack.

Years go by, as the starship continues on at a little over a trillion miles an hour. Dr. George Benson, aboard the starship, has now reached his life expectancy of 100 years, so it is time for him to go into the rejuvenation machine. He goes into the metal cabinet of the machine, and throws the switches. Red, green and yellow lights flash on and off, accompanied by a loud whining noise that changes into a high-pitched screech. A half-hour later, Benson steps out of the cabinet looking like a young man and ready for another lifetime.

More years pass and the spaceship traveling at 1500 times the speed of light approached the first star of the galaxy. It had taken thirty-eight years to reach this galaxy, whereas, if they had been traveling at just the speed of light, it would have taken tens of thousands of years. The plan was not to stop at any of the stars, but to criss-cross this galaxy.

The recreation area of the spaceship contains beautiful parks with trees, green grass, lakes and ponds. Queen Virena and Captain York talked as they strolled through this lovely area of the ship.

"I see that Zorax has conquered dozens of solar systems and his warship fleets number into the millions," said Virena.

"Wow!" exclaimed York. "That sounds so unbelievable, but knowing the powers of your mind, I know it must be true. And also, knowing the character of Zorax, I can believe it."

"I see Zorax, now coming into another solar system with ten planets revolving around the star. There are three planets in this system, with living beings on them. Zorax has gone into orbit around one of these planets. He is in the warship with the super powerful beam gun. He aims at the planet and fires. The whole planet is blown apart and three and a half billion people on the planet have been killed," exclaims Virena, as she tells York of the vision she is seeing.

"My God, that's horrible," cries York.

"Zorax has now sent a message to the people of the other two planets, that if they don't surrender right away, they will get the same treatment," said Virena. The troubled York and Queen Virena talk a little longer and then both return to their apartments.

Years go by and the Aon starship is halfway across this galaxy. In the recreation section of the ship is a gymnasium, built jointly by the Aons and the Earthlings, at the request of the Earthlings. The gymnasium is designed for various exercises, including a basketball court built according to the Earthling's specifications.

Suddenly, a voice crackles over the intercom, "Atheasis to the bridge! Atheasis to the bridge!"

Upon hearing her name, Atheasis quickly excused herself and rushed to the bridge.

"What is going on?" asked Atheasis as she reached the bridge.

"We have spotted three vessels just ahead of us. Would you like me to do a full scan on them?" asks Trais.

"Yes, please," answers Atheasis.

"I sure hope they're not warships," said Barthena.

As the scanners are activated, they make a pulsating sound and flash yellow lights.

"They are slow-moving ships going at sub-light speed," reports Trais, "indicating that the vessels are not warships or pirate ships. There is a supply ship, a freighter and a trading ship, all three unarmed." "I'm sure glad of that, because we have very few weapons aboard," said Barthena.

"There are 97 persons on board the freighter—50 males and 47 females," reports Trais. "The trading ship has fifty-four males and fifty females, and on the supply ship, there are sixty-two males and sixty-three females. All three ships are of the ion propulsion system,"

“Whew,” sighs Barthena, “I’m sure glad they’re unarmed vessels.”

The other two women quickly agree to that. The Aon starship soon overtook the three ships, and because they are going at the tremendous speed of 1500 times the speed of light, they soon left the three ships behind.

The Aon starship has criss-crossed this galaxy and is now heading for the next one. It has taken them fourteen years to span this galaxy.

Chapter XIX THE SEARCH FOR LIFE

It has taken 137 years to reach the next galaxy and the Aon starship is approaching the first star of this galaxy. The Aon women pilots and Captain York are at the bridge. The starship has been steadily slowing down as it nears the star. From their vantage point, York and the Aon women are able to detect ten planets revolving around the star. The ship continues its deceleration as it heads toward the outer planet of this solar system. Atheasis gives the order to bypass the outer planets and to head for the inner planets. As they are checking out the planets, they have started using their anti-magnetic system, which uses the magnetic fields of the planets for power. Top speed for these engines is 10,000,000 miles an hour. These engines are very versatile, capable of great speeds, slow speeds, or even hovering. The ship has now gone into orbit around the planet.

"Okay, turn on the scanners and we will check this planet out," said Atheasis.

"All right," answered Trais.

Once more, as the scanners are activated, there is the familiar pulsating sound and flashing yellow light. The scanners can tell almost everything about the planet's surface—temperature, pressure, and whether there is any life on the surface. The scanners could even detect microscopic life. There are screens on board, which give a panoramic view of the planet's surface. The starship went into orbit 1000 miles above the planet. The temperature is recorded at 1000 degrees and the pressure is 100 atmospheres, according to Trais.

"Well, take us out of orbit then, Trais, and give full power to the antimagnetic engines," said Atheasis.

As they head toward the next planet, York asks Atheasis, "If we find no livable planet at this solar system and we set course for another one, will we continue at just the speed of light, or will we be able to continue at 1500 times the speed of light?"

"We are able to store up some of the power we gained from the interstellar gas clouds, and therefore, we can still maintain 1500 times the speed of light," answers Atheasis.

"How long can we go on the stored cloud power?" asks York.

"We can land on, or orbit, all of the planets of a certain solar system and when we revert back to the stored cloud power, that counts as one time. We can revert back to the stored cloud power 25 different times before we run out and have to find more clouds again," said Atheasis.

"Wow," exclaimed York. "We can sure go a heck of a distance before we have to search for gas clouds again."

Atheasis nodded in response.

Quiet returns to the bridge as they continue toward the next planet, which they reach a few hours later. The scanners are turned on once again. A beam goes down to the planet's surface, indicating that scanning is taking place. It was soon learned that poisonous gases were on the planet's surface, making it unlivable. It was proven that all the planets of this system were uninhabitable, because of heat, cold, or some other inhospitable factor. Atheasis gave the order to go out of orbit and go full power to the anti-magnetic engines. Then shortly, she gave the order for full power to the photon-drive engines, and they were soon up to light speed. A few hours later, she gave the order for full power from the stored cloud power engines, and they were once again up to over a trillion miles an hour. In about twenty-five hours, they had reached another star. They discovered that there were six planets revolving around this star. The ship slowed down, and immediately they started scanning these planets. They soon found that this solar system, like the one before, had no livable planets.

Once again, the order was given to leave the solar system. They were soon back to their maximum speed and after another thirty hours they reached another solar system, but after another scanning check of the five planets in the system, they again found that none were livable. So, once again, they were headed for another system.

Upon their arrival there, three days later, they were disappointed to find that there were no livable planets there, either.

Back at the bridge, First Officer Simpson is talking to the beautiful Aon women. “I certainly have to admit that I’m getting very anxious to find a life-supporting planet,” he said.

“I can understand why you are becoming so anxious, Russ, but it just could be that we might not find a livable planet in this galaxy,” said Atheasis.

“I know, of course, there is really nothing to worry about, since we have the rejuvenation machines, but I still can’t help being anxious to find a planet on which to settle,” said Russ.

“You never know,” said Barthena, “the very next star might have a livable revolving around it.”

“I sure hope so,” said Russ.

“I have to admit that I have the same feelings,” said Trais. Russ then left the women pilots to carry on their duties.

Chapter XX THE METALLICS

The Aon starship continued on its journey at over a trillion miles an hour and finally reached another star. The ship didn't stop, or even slow down, as they found that there were no planets around it, but only nine smaller stars revolving around the big star. It was a solar system of stars.

After about another week, they reach another star, which they find has nine planets revolving around it. Atheasis gives the order to slow down in preparation for entering the solar system. As they enter the system, they convert back to their anti-magnetic engines. They bypass the four outer planets and set a course for the inner planets.

Atheasis gave the order to slow down and go into orbit around the first of the inner planets. They go into orbit a thousand miles above the planet. Trais immediately turns on the ship's scanners to check out the planet's surface. Once again, accompanied by the pulsating sound and flashing lights, a panoramic view of the planet is shown on the screen.

"The scanners show that this is another hostile planet with poisonous gas on the surface," said Trais.

"All right, take us out of orbit and full power to the anti-magnetic engines," said Atheasis.

"What heading would you like?" asked Barthena.

"Just make a heading for the next planet," answered Atheasis.

A few hours later, the Aon ship reaches the next planet and goes into orbit around it at about the same height as at the last planet.

The scanners are again activated and Trais remarks to Jack Harrison, who is visiting on the bridge, "The planet shows to be a life-supporting planet, but it would not be advisable to land."

"I don't understand. If it's a life-supporting planet, why can't we land?" asked Jack.

"Well, it appears to be a very unstable planet," Trais answered.

"Why is it unstable?" asks Atheasis.

"The planet has no rotation, and if we were to go in for a landing, the planet might shortly afterward crumble into pieces," said Trais.

"What could have caused the planet to stop rotating?" asked Jack.

"There are several giant planets in this solar system, and sometime in the system's history all of the planets lined up. This caused the smaller planet's rotation to slow down and eventually, to stop," explained Trais.

"I can understand that, all right," answered Jack.

Atheasis gave the order to take the ship out of orbit and to check all of the other planets of the system. As the hours slipped into days, they found that there were no planets in this system on which they could land. So full power was given to the anti-magnetic engines until they had passed the furthest planet in this system. Atheasis then gave orders for full power to the photon-drive engines, and they were soon up to the speed of light. She shortly gave the order to switch to the stored-cloud power engines, and they were soon up to their maximum speed of 1500 times the speed of light.

Five more days pass before the starship reaches another solar system. They find that this star has five planets revolving around it. They slow down and go into orbit around the first planet. As they scan this planet, they find it to be life supporting. They are soon to find that the planet is called Verian. The scanners indicate that there are living beings on its surface.

"According to our scanners and sensors, it seems that these beings have a metallic outer skin," said Trais. "It sounds like they are robots," remarked Captain York.

"No, they are not robots, but living creatures," said Trais.

"But how could that be?" asked York. "It breaks all laws of biology."

"All we know is that for some reason, the chemistry of their bodies causes the outer skin to be metallic. Otherwise, they are normal, living, breathing beings," said Trais.

"That is very strange," said York. "Yet, in a way, I can understand it," said First Officer Russell Simpson.

"Creatures back on Earth, such as turtles and armadillos have hard shells on the outside, and some insects had exoskeletons."

"Well, that is certainly another way of looking at it. These creatures just have metal outer skin rather than the bony material we were used to on Earth," said York, "but, it still blows my mind."

"I have to admit that it's unusual for me too," said Barthena.

Trais and Atheasis quickly agreed.

"Are we going to land?" asked Russ.

"We will not land until we get a more complete report on the population levels and find out just what those people are like," said Atheasis.

Suddenly, an image with voice appeared on the ship's screen, "I am Elion, the leader of the race of Verians. We know of your orbit around our planet and wish to know your intentions." Elion's voice had a weird vibrating sound.

"I am Atheasis, Captain of this starship. We come in peace and wish no harm to your people. We were forced to leave our solar system, because of a warlike race called the Aldans, whose leader was called Zorax," said Atheasis. "Since we left our solar system, we have been searching for a livable planet on which to settle."

"I'm sorry to hear of your misfortune, but it is our policy not to allow any colonization of our planet, no matter how peaceful the prospective colonizers might be. We must ask you to leave our planet and our solar system immediately. If you attempt a landing on our planet, we will be forced to destroy your ship and all aboard," said Elion.

"All right, I understand your feelings. We will leave immediately," said Atheasis.

She then gave orders for full power to the anti-magnetic engines and, after a few hours, they were on photon-drive and soon at the speed of light. They quickly left this solar system behind.

Chapter XXI THE PIRATES

A short time later, Atheasis and Trais are talking. "Our scanners show that there is a lot of debris in space for the next five light years, so it wouldn't be advisable to go full power to our stored cloud power," reports Trais.

"All right, get a computer readout as to what would be a safe speed for us," said Atheasis.

"Okay," replied Trais.

A few minutes later, Trais reports that the computers indicate that ten times the speed of light should be our top speed.

"We will go at just that speed, then," said Atheasis, "but keep me posted on our progress."

Trais and Barthena both nodded that they understood.

Captain York who was on the bridge with the beautiful Aon women, remarked, "That sounds very scary, the fact that we could collide with matter in space."

"It is," said Atheasis, "but there is nothing to worry about as long as we travel not more than ten times the speed of light."

"Well, that's reassuring," said Dick, and then, changing the subject, he asked, "How knowledgeable are you of this galaxy?"

"We know very little. We have done some mapping and we know of a few star constellations, but for the most part, we know very little about it," said Atheasis.

Trais breaks into their conversation with, "The scanners show that there are four vessels ahead of us."

"What kind of ships are they?" asks Atheasis.

"They are well-armed pirate ships and are powered by vitron engines," answers Trais.

"Oh, no," cries Barthena.

"What speed are they traveling?" asks Atheasis.

"They are below light speed," Trais said.

Atheasis and the others on the bridge gave a sigh of relief at that news.

"I sure hope they don't chase after us," said Barthena.

They all had the same thoughts. Soon, the Aon starship pulled alongside of the four vessels and zipped on by, leaving them quickly behind.

"Look!" said Barthena, pointing at the ship's screen, "It's Zicon."

"Who's Zicon?" asked York.

"He is a pirate and scavenger from our galaxy," said Atheasis. "What I would like to know is what he is doing in this galaxy. He has always stayed in area 6 of our galaxy. He used to raid many of our supply and mining ships, so that we stayed clear of that area."

"The pirate ships have increased their speed to just the speed of light," reports Trais. "Shall we speed up?"

"No, maintain our present speed, but keep me posted on every move they make," said Atheasis.

A short time later, Trais reports that the pirates have increased to ten times the speed of light and asks if Atheasis wishes to increase speed.

"No," replies Atheasis.

"Well, the chase is sure on now," said York.

Minutes tick by and Trais reports that the pirates are now at fifty times the speed of light and closing fast.

"All right, increase our speed to 75 times the speed of light," said Atheasis.

"Why! This is utter insanity," said Barthena. "We'll all be killed."

This was what everyone on the bridge was thinking. It was a tough decision for Atheasis to make, and there was a look of absolute terror on the faces of those witnessing this turn of events.

"It looks like no choice we have is very desirable," said York. "If we slow down, we'll be captured and probably killed by the pirates. The more we speed up, the more chance we have of crashing into the debris."

Trais reports that the pirates are now at 100 times light speed. Atheasis then gave the order to increase to 125 times the speed of light.

"I can't stand much more of this. It will be a miracle if we get through this area alive," declared Barthena.

"If my memory serves me right, the top speed of the vitron engine is 100 times light speed," said Trais.

"I think you're right, Trais," said Atheasis.

"Then their engines will get hot if they try to match our speed, now," said Trais.

"That's the best news yet, unless they have modified and developed those engines for better speed," said Barthena.

"Well, let's hope they haven't," said Atheasis.

Those good feelings were soon dashed as Trais reported that the pirate ships were up to 140 times light speed and closing in on them rapidly. Everyone on the bridge was cast into a state of utter terror.

"This is absolute insanity," said Barthena, as Atheasis quickly gave the order to increase the speed to 150 times light speed. In a short time, Trais reported that the pirate ships had achieved the same speed.

"All right, get us up to 175," ordered Atheasis.

"Okay," replies Trais, with a frightened sound in her voice. They continue on at this tremendous speed, with the pirate ships still chasing them.

"Have they increased their speed?" asks Atheasis.

"No," answers Trais. "In fact, their engines are heating badly. They are super hot right now. If they try to maintain this speed much longer, their ships will blow up."

Smiles lit up the faces of those on the bridge.

"One of the pirate ship's engines has blown up and the ship has vaporized into nothingness. The others are slowing down," reports Trais.

"They are down to 140-125-100 times the speed of light. I see a flash. One of the ships has been hit by a meteor and has blown into pieces."

Atheasis then gave the order to start gradually to slow down.

"They are now down to 86 times light speed," exclaimed Trais.

"Wow! This is great! We've really got them now," cried Captain York.

"Yes, we are safe now from the pirate ships, but we still have a tough job ahead of us, just getting safely through this area," said Atheasis.

"Well, I feel confident we will get through all right, now. You have done a tremendous job," remarked York.

"That surely makes me feel good to hear that," said Atheasis. York then leaves the bridge and returns to his apartment.

Days of great tension slip by, but finally, they are through the area of debris. Atheasis then gives the order to accelerate the stored cloud power, and they are, once again, up to their top speed of over a trillion miles an hour.

Twenty-five hours later, the starship approaches another star, which proves to have six planets revolving around it. They slow down and switch to the anti-magnetic engines as they near the first planet. Trais immediately activates the scanners, and a panoramic view of the planet appears on the screen. It shows a bleak, hostile planet, with mountains, valleys, and plains. The atmosphere is far too thin to be livable, so Atheasis orders them out of orbit and full power to the anti-magnetic engines. Hours later they reach the next planet and go into orbit around it. The scanners show not only mountains and valleys, but also cities on the planet's surface.

"At last! We've finally found a life-supporting planet. When do we land?" asked Barthena, excitedly.

"Not so fast," said Trais. "We can't land."

"Why not?" asks Atheasis.

"Well, it's true that we've found a life-supporting planet, but it is so overcrowded that there is a being for every square foot of surface," said Trais.

"How can they possibly survive under such circumstances?" asked Atheasis.

"They do it with their mile-high spiral buildings," said Trais.

They reluctantly left the planet's orbit and headed for the next planet. This one, too, proved to be very hostile, with a surface temperature of minus 150 degrees and winds of 1500 miles an hour. They again took their departure and were soon sailing silently and serenely through the blackness of space at 10,000,000 miles an hour. They traveled for two more days before reaching the next planet and going into orbit around it. The scanners soon proved to be ineffective because of the terrible dust storms on the planet's surface. Eight hours pass as they continue to orbit the planet in hope that the dust would clear. At that moment, two ships appear on the ship's screen. One was just ahead of them and the other to one side. The crew quickly identified them as the pirate ships that they had earlier out-raced.

Zicon soon appeared on the screen saying, "All of our weapons are aimed at you and we demand that you prepare your ship for immediate boarding."

"What shall we do?" asks Trais.

"Well, since we have very few weapons, and it would be difficult to escape, we'll just have to let them come on board," replied Atheasis.

Shortly, Zicon and his comrades boarded the Aon starship with drawn beam pistols and went directly to the bridge. Six of his cohorts were with Zicon. They were a strange looking bunch with only one leg apiece, one threatening eye in the middle of their forehead. They did have the usual number of arms, noses, ears and mouths that the Earthlings were used to. The creatures were about six feet tall or a little over. When they moved on the one leg, it was in a scooting fashion, as if by some kind of propulsion. When the pirates reached the bridge, they found not only Atheasis, Trais, and Barthena, but also, Queen Virena and Captain York. The seven pirates aimed their beam pistols at the Aons and one Earthman.

"Okay, I'll just take that jeweled necklace from you," Zicon said to Queen Virena, in his high shrill voice.

"I can't let you have it. It's very valuable and a symbol of my power as queen," said Virena.

"Give it to me right now!" said Zicon more menacingly.

"You'd better give it to him, Virena," said York. With that, Queen Virena quickly, but reluctantly, surrendered the beautiful, jeweled necklace to Zicon. The rest of the victims gave to the pirates anything they considered to be of value. Then Zicon, leaving two of his comrades on the bridge, went with the other four pirates through the rest of the starship until they had robbed from all 560 persons on board. He then ordered the air locks to be opened, so that he and his men could depart.

As the pirates were leaving, Atheasis asked, “Why have you left us with nothing?”

Zicon answered in almost an identical way as Attilla the Hun had, centuries before when he had sacked Rome, “I have left you with your lives, which I don’t always do.”

Chapter XXII THE DISEASED PLANETS

Soon after Zicon's attack on them, the Aon starship had left that solar system and was back up to their maximum speed of one-sixth of a light year an hour. About thirty hours later, they reached another system and found that there were three planets revolving around the star. The first two proved to be not hospitable for life, so they went on to the third one. They went into orbit around it and Trais turned on the scanners. When the panoramic view came on the screen, the Aon pilots were confronted with a horrible sight. There were bodies all over, and they were smoking and smoldering. The buildings seemed to be intact with no fire or smoking.

“Do you think there was a terrible fire on the planet?” asked Atheasis.

“No, our scanners and sensors show that these people are dying of a terrible disease, involving their metabolism, which is causing them to literally burn up from the inside out,” said Trais.

“Well, that is certainly a strange disease,” said Atheasis.

“Do you think we could contract it if we were among them?” asked Barthena.

“It’s hard to tell, for sure, maybe we would and maybe we wouldn’t, but I would say there is no reason to take the chance. I would strongly advise that we leave orbit immediately,” said Trais.

The other two women agreed, so they went full power to their antimagnetic engines until they had passed the last planet in the solar system. They then went full power photon drive, followed shortly by full power to the stored cloud power engines, and so, were soon up to 1500 times the speed of light.

Three more days pass and the Aon starship is approaching yet another star. They slow down as they approach and are able to see that there are twelve planets around it. They then go into orbit around the first planet, and Trais is again at the scanners. It is soon learned that the planet is much too cold for life, so they leave this planet. About eight hours later, they near the next planet and go into orbit around it. After making only one circuit, the scanners show that this planet, too, is inhospitable because of tremendous heat.

The group continues on to the inner planets, the first of which they reach in about twelve hours after the hot planet. They go into orbit and Jack Harrison, who is on the bridge with the Aon women, watches as Trais gleans information about the planet from the scanners and sensors. She reports that there is a race of people on the planet, but they are dying very quickly.

"What are they dying of?" asks Atheasis.

"The information I am receiving indicates that they are dying of a strange disease which causes them to become younger and younger," answers Trais.

"How does that make them die?" asks Jack.

"Well, it seems to affect only the adult population, which becomes younger, going back to childhood, infancy, and then back to an embryo and death," answers Trais.

"This is absolutely amazing," said Jack. "I have never heard of such a fantastic thing. Would there be any chance of the Earthlings or Aons catching such a disease?"

"Well, we don't really know, because up to now, we had never heard of the disease either. However, I would say that we must not take such a chance, as I am responsible for all 560 persons aboard this ship," said Atheasis.

"I don't think that we Aons or you Earthlings would be affected in the same way as these people, but nevertheless, we could be affected in a different, but perhaps just as horrible a way," said Trais.

"Is there any way we could help those people?" asked Jack.

"Since we are so unfamiliar with the disease, it would take some time for us to devise an antidote, and therefore, it would be too late," said Trais.

"Not only that, we run the risk of being exposed ourselves," answers Barthena.

The starship then leaves the orbit of the diseased planet, but finds the rest of the planets are unlivable, so they head out of this solar system. They are soon up to the maximum speed of a trillion miles (1/6 of a light year) an hour.

Chapter XXIII THE MONSTERS

A week later, the Aon starship reached the next star, where they found eight planets revolving around it. After scanning and rejecting several of the planets, they have at last found one that appears to be life supporting. All 560 persons aboard the starship are in a state of jubilation at hearing this news. The huge, mile in diameter, ship glides slowly into the atmosphere for a landing. As they touch down, they find themselves in a clearing surrounded by a steaming jungle. The Aon women on the bridge, along with York, Simpson, and Harrison, are looking out the windows at the steaming jungle scene.

"Isn't it great that after traveling hundreds of thousands of light years beyond Proxima Centauri and in the middle of another galaxy that we have finally found another planet on which to settle?" said Russ.

"Yes, it sure is, and another good thing about it is the fact that there is no other race living on the planet that we might be in conflict with," said Jack.

"You know, it is rather strange that even though this is a life-supporting planet that there aren't people living here," said Dick.

"Well, all I've go to say is, what are we waiting for? Let's get out of the ship and enjoy our newfound world," said Simpson.

"I certainly see no reason to stay in the ship any longer, but I'll ask Atheasis if there is anything we might have to do before disembarking," said York.

When York asked Atheasis about leaving the ship, she replied that all that was left to do was to check a couple of computer readouts and then they'd be ready to step out on the planet's surface. There was much handshaking and smiling on the faces of the passengers when they learned that they would soon be exploring their new home. Russ glanced out the window and saw a strange creature in the clearing a short distance from the ship.

"Will you look at the size of that creature out there," cried Russ.

"What are you talking about?" asked Trais. "Our scanners showed that there was no animal life on the planet."

"Well, come and look for yourself," said Russ.

York, Harrison, and the Aon women rushed up to the window and looked out. They, too, saw what Russ had seen. The creature was truly gigantic, standing 486 feet tall. It was covered with a combination of scales and feathers, and had a long goose neck and a triangular head. As far as the spectators could see, the creature had a mouth, but no eyes or ears. It did have an antenna-like devise on top of its head.

"Maybe you'd better check the computers, scanners, and sensors to see if they are working properly," Atheasis said to Trais.

"All right, I'll check them over," answered Trais.

Just at that moment, the creature let out a horrible screech, making the whole ship vibrate. He then started walking toward the ship.

"Do you suppose he's coming to attack us?" asked Simpson.

"I sure don't know what his intentions are, but he could have that in mind," said York.

"It could be that he might be friendly," said Jack.

"Well, I guess we'll soon know," exclaimed Barthena.

A short time later, Trais returned, saying, "All of the computers seem to be working all right."

"Then, why are we seeing this monster?" asked York.

"I've got a theory that he may make himself exist and then non-exist at will," said Trais.

"Wow! That defies all known laws of nature," said York.

"The way I look at it," said Russ, "there are worlds out among the stars with life that is entirely different and with powers that are incomprehensible to us."

Silence then settled over the ship, with everyone on board watching as the big creature walked ever closer to the ship.

"What is that big object in the monster's mouth?" asked Jack, but none could answer his question.

The object was egg-shaped, black, and weighed about 2 ½ tons. Suddenly, the object was catapulted out of the creature's mouth, crashing into the side of the ship. The ship shook violently.

"My God! I've never seen anything like this," said York.

"Well, one thing we know now, is that he isn't friendly," said Jack.

The creature shot another missile out of its mouth with a horrible screech, and made the ship vibrate again.

"The way I look at the situation, the only thing preventing our settling on this planet is this beast. If we can kill him, we'll be home free," said York. "What kind of weapons do be have aboard?"

"Well, we've got three beam rifles, two beam pistols, and a beam cannon," answered Atheasis.

Once again, the monster sent one of his weapons into the side of the ship with a loud crash.

"I'll take Jack and Russ with me and we'll go out and kill the monster," said York.

"I sure would hate to see you go out there. I would be scared for your lives," said Atheasis.

"He is the only thing that stands in the way of our settling on this planet, and if we don't kill him soon he will destroy the ship," exclaimed York.

"Okay, but let me send a couple of my people to help," said Atheasis.

York quickly accepted the offer and disembarked with his helpers. Dick, Russ, and Jack took the beam rifles, and the two Aon men sent along to help, had the pistols.

"My God, the size of that monster chills me right to the bone," said Russ.

None of the other men disagreed with Russ.

"Are you guys ready?" asked York.

"I think we're about as ready as we'll ever be," answered Jack.

"All right. When I give the signal, we will fire our guns all at the same time," said York.

With that they all aimed their weapons at the monster and when York gave the order, they fired simultaneously and continued for fully five minutes.

"I don't believe it. With full beam gun power we didn't even faze him," said Russ.

Just at that moment, the monster fired another object, which sailed over the men's heads and landed just behind them. He fired again, this time hitting the ship.

"What do you say to our continuing to fire our guns at him and maybe eventually it may get to him," said York.

They agreed and started firing at the monster, once more. The monster disappeared.

"What do you suppose happened? Do you think we killed him?" asked Russ.

"I don't know, but I sure hope so," answered York.

But, they suddenly heard again the now familiar loud screech that shook the ground under them. They looked around and found that the creature had reappeared on the right side of them. They fired their guns at him and he disappeared and reappeared again, this time on the left side. Beams started to issue from its antennas.

"Let's get back to the ship. We can't kill the monster. He is using the very beams from our guns against us," said York.

The men agreed and started toward the ship. As they were running, the creature shot another black object that crashed into the ship's side. Then he immediately shot another toward the running men. It hit the ground before reaching them and started rolling toward them. All of the men were able to get out of its way except First Officer Russell Simpson. The big, 2½ ton object hit Russ, rolled over him and continued rolling. Simpson lay motionless on the ground as the other men approached him.

"Oh, my God! Russ! Russ! Please wake up," cried York. There was no sound or movement from Russ.

"Look, the monster is rushing at us. What shall we do?" asked Jack. "We certainly can't leave Russ here."

"No, we will not do that," said Dick.

The two Aon men then took charge, and with their mind control lifted the body of Russ into the air and across the ground. The other men quickly followed toward the ship as the monster continued to chase them.

As the men approached, Atheasis ordered the ship's door to be opened. The door with steps touched the ground and Russ was the first to reach it, and he sailed into the ship with the other men following right behind. When they were all in, the door clanged shut. Russ was gently laid on one of the ship's couches and was immediately attended by Dr. Benson, Nurse Sacks and the Aon doctors and nurses.

The monster had stopped a short distance from the ship, and he now fired another of his black objects against the ship, making it shake violently. Atheasis quickly ordered immediate departure from the planet. Before the ship could leave the ground, the passengers saw five more of the creatures. Full antimagnetic power was applied, and the planet and monsters were quickly left behind and the ship was soon out in the blackness of space once again. Russ was rushed to sick bay where he immediately underwent surgery. A few hours later, Dr. Benson came out of the operating room to report to York on Russ's condition.

"Well, I hate to give you such bad news, but your First Officer is in very bad shape. Practically every bone in his body is broken, and he has internal injuries. He is in a coma, and I'm afraid he doesn't have much chance of coming through this alive," said Benson.

"Oh my God! This is terrible. I shouldn't have exposed all of us to such danger. We could have always gone to another star and found a livable planet," said York, guiltily.

"Don't blame yourself. We all felt that this was our opportunity," said George.

"What about the rejuvenation machine? Would that fix Russ?" asked Dick.

"No, I've already asked Atheasis, and she said it was just good for repairing damage from aging, not injuries," said Benson.

"What are we going to do? I hope someway, somehow that Russ will snap out of it," said Dick.

"Well, I do too, and I can assure you that we will all do our best to bring Russ back to normal," said Dr. Benson.

"I know you will," said Captain York.

"I'd better get back to my patient," said Dr. Benson as he left York.

Chapter XXIV THE PLANET OF FEAR

Several days have passed since the Aon starship left the last solar system and they are now back to the maximum speed of over a trillion miles an hour.

First Officer Russell Simpson is still near death in sick bay aboard the ship. Captain York, Dr. Benson, and Nurse Sacks, very concerned about Russ, are discussing his condition.

"How is he doing?" asked York.

"There has been no change. He is still in a coma," replied Dr. Benson.

"What are his chances?" asked York.

"I hate to sound so negative, but they are not too good," answered Benson.

"But, we're not giving up on him, and someway we'll bring him out of it. Right, Doctor?" soothed Nurse Sacks.

"Right, Susan, of course we'll never stop trying," said Benson.

"Would it be all right for me to go down to see him?" asked York.

"No, I'm sorry, Dick, but it just wouldn't be advisable right now. He is critical, but I'll keep you posted on any change," said the doctor.

"All right," York reluctantly agreed.

"I'll say one thing though, that should give us a ray of hope," said Dr. Benson,

"these Aon doctors and nurses are absolutely tremendous. I really envy their tremendous technology and medicines."

"I certainly agree with you," said Susan.

"Well, that's good to hear," said York.

"Have you heard any reports as to the damage to the ship?" asked Benson, changing the subject.

"As a matter of fact, I have. Atheasis told me that there was just minor damage. There are big dents on the outside, but no damage to any vital equipment," said York.

"Well, that's sure good news," said Dr. Benson. The doctor and nurse then excused themselves to return to Russ.

A few hours later, Trais, on the bridge reported, "Our scanners have detected six vessels just ahead of us."

"What kind of ships are they?" asked Atheasis.

"They are well-armed warships," replied Trais.

"Oh no!" cried Barthena.

"What is their speed?" Atheasis asked.

"They are traveling at 100 times the speed of light," reported Trais.

"If they can't go any faster than that, we sure don't have to worry about them," said Atheasis, "but, we'll soon know."

Shortly the Aon ship passed the other vessels.

"Have they increased their speed?" asked Atheasis.

"Yes, they are now at 125 times the speed of light," said Trais.

"All right, keep me continually informed on them," ordered Atheasis.

"I sure will," agreed Trais.

"I sure hope they can't keep up with us," worried Barthena.

Trais then reported that the six vessels were up to 150 times light speed.

"Well, there's no question now that they are chasing us," said Atheasis.

"They are now at 200 times light speed," reported Trais, "now 250."

"They still have a long way to go before reaching our speed," said Atheasis, "but, that's no assurance that they can't reach our speed or even more."

Trais soon reported that the alien vessels had reached 500 times light speed.

"Is there any indication that their engines are heating up?" asked Atheasis.

"No," answered Trais, "but, they are now up to 750 times the speed of light and increasing."

"Well, they're up to half our maximum speed right now and I hope they can't go any faster," said Barthena.

"They can go faster because they're already up to 850 times light speed," reported Trais.

"Is there any indication yet that their engines are heating up?" asked Atheasis.

"There is still no indication of that," answered Trais. "In fact, they are now at a thousand times the speed of light."

Looks of real worry and fear appeared on the faces of the Aon women.

"I think we may not have cause to worry," remarked Trais, "as the scanners show that their engines are now starting to heat up and now they show very hot."

Cheers rose from the group of Aon ladies on the bridge.

"I'm afraid you're a little premature with your cheering," remarked Trais. "We're not rid of those warships yet, even though their engines are heating, because they've managed to raise their speed to 1250 times light speed."

"Do you think we can outrun them?" asked Barthena.

"Yes, I believe we can, because even though they were able to gain speed, somehow in doing this, their engines have become super hot," said Trais.

"Then we've got them, but we're not going to make the mistake we did the last time, passing a half a dozen stars before we start looking for a life-supporting planet," said Atheasis.

"Two of the warships' engines have blown up on them, and the others have started slowing down," reported Trais.

"Wow, this is great," cheered Barthena, with the other two Aon women joining in.

A couple of days later, Captain York is talking to Dr. Benson, who says, "Well, Dick, I've got great news for you. I think your First Mate is going to make it."

"That is great news, all right. Can you tell me more?"

"Well, he has come out of the coma. He's still a little groggy, but that's to be expected after what he's gone through. He is in good spirits, though," said Dr. Benson. "To be absolutely frank with you, Dick, I didn't think Russ had a chance. I have to give all the credit to the fine Aon medical staff. They performed a near miracle."

"How soon will you let him out of sick bay?" asked Dick.

"We're going to keep him here for at least another week to make sure that he's all right," said the doctor.

"Can I go down to see him?" asked York.

"Yes, I think that would be all right, but only stay a few minutes," cautioned Dr. Benson.

Dick left quickly to go visit his old friend. When he came to Simpson's room, he called out, "How are all these doctors and nurses treating you?"

"Oh, pretty good," replied Russ, "but, I can't wait to get out of here."

"Take it easy. We sure don't want to lose you now," said York.

"You don't have to worry about that, Dick. I'm tough as nails and you'll see me out of here in no time," said Russ.

Dick gave a little laugh, "You're probably right."

Then a smile came over Russ's face. "Can you promise me one thing, though?" asked Russ.

"What's that?" York asked.

"Well, just promise me that we won't have to fight any more horrible, undefeatable monsters," Russ said, with a chuckle.

Dick also chuckled and said, "I can definitely say that we will not try that again. In fact, if we ever land on another planet with such beasts and they even look at us in a mean way, we'll leave."

"That sounds good," said Russ just as Nurse Sacks entered the room and told Dick that he would have to leave so that Russ could get some rest.

Six weeks have passed since the Aons and Earthlings left the last solar system. They have passed six stars, and are now approaching the seventh. First Officer Russell Simpson is out of sick bay and back to normal. Atheasis gives the order to slow down for the approaching star. As they draw nearer, they see that there are nine planets revolving around the star. Captain York, First Officer Russell Simpson, and Navigator Jack Harrison are on the bridge with the Aon women pilots.

A sudden fear grips Harrison and he cries, “Please, let’s not stop at any of these planets in this solar system.”

“Why not?” asks York.

“All I know is that I feel a terrible fear that if we stop at this solar system, we will all be destroyed,” said Jack.

Both York and Simpson said that they didn’t feel any fear.

“How about you, Atheasis? Do you feel the fear that Jack does?” asked York. Atheasis answered in the negative as did Trais and Barthena.

“I can’t understand your having such an overwhelming fear, Jack,” said Dick.

“I can’t either, Dick, but I do and it’s getting worse. I suppose you think I’m crazy,” moaned Jack.

“No, I don’t think you’re crazy, Jack. It may be caused by some phenomenon that we can’t understand,” said Dick.

Simpson agreed with York’s reasoning.

“Do you think the fear Jack is feeling could be caused by one of the planets of this solar system, Atheasis?” asked York.

"It could be possible. I can sure check out the planets and find out," said Atheasis.

"No, please don't! Let's just continue on and skip this solar system," begged Jack.

It now became apparent to everyone on the bridge that Jack was literally shaking with fear.

"Take it easy, Jack. We can soon find out what is causing your fear," said Russ.

Dick and Russ tried everything they could think of to try to calm Jack, but to no avail. His fear just became more intense until he became absolutely hysterical. In fact, they had a hard time in restraining him. Atheasis called for doctors and nurses to come to the bridge and escort Jack to sick bay. When he had been removed from the bridge, Atheasis gave the order to continue on to this solar system. As they drew nearer to the solar system, the same fear that Jack had, overcame Dick and Russ, and they were soon in a state of hysteria and had to be taken to sick bay as Jack had been.

Atheasis continued on toward the solar system, as she wanted to get to the bottom of this strange phenomenon. The Aon women all wondered if one of the planets was, indeed, causing the terrible fear in the Earthmen. The fear had soon expanded until all of the Earth people on board were affected by it, but none of the Aon men or women had come under its influence. The Aon starship soon came to the first planet of the solar system and went into orbit around it. The scanners were immediately activated and showed that this planet was not life supporting, so they headed for the next planet. There had still been no clues about the strange fear, which was rampant on the ship. Upon arrival at the second planet, the scanners were quickly turned on.

"I have picked up some strong signals from the planet," said Trais.

"Can you make out what they are?" asked Atheasis.

"Yes, they are thought transmissions from the planet and according to the scanners and my computer readouts, they show that there are beings on the planet who are sending out the very transmissions which caused the terrible fear in the Earth people," reported Trais, "It was their way of trying to keep us from landing on their planet and do it without violence."

"Do you think that if we went on in for a landing that they would destroy us and our ship?" asked Atheasis.

"Yes, I do," answered Trais.

"Then, let's leave," said Atheasis.

"Do you want me to set a course to check out the other planets of the system?" asked Barthena.

Atheasis said that they should do so, but they found upon checking all of the system's planets, that none were livable, so they abandoned this system.

Chapter XXV THE INTERSTELLAR SPACE BUGS

Twenty-five hours later, the Aon spaceship traveling at its maximum speed of over a trillion miles an hour, approaches another star, but they soon find that they can not stop there. The reason is that it has gone nova. The Aon women are on the bridge, and Trais has turned on the scanners.

"How far out has the star expanded?" asked Atheasis.

"According to my readouts, I figure it has expanded out 100 times its original size," said Trais and added, "There are still six planets orbiting around the star."

"Well, one thing we can be pretty sure of, is that if there ever was life on those planets, there isn't now," said Barthena.

"Are we far enough away to be safe from the star?" asked Atheasis.

"Right now we are, but as we pass by it, we will have to do a heading of 2 . 6 . 8 to be at a safe distance," answered Barthena.

"Let's start on that heading immediately, then," said Atheasis.

"Okay," said Barthena. As they went by the star, the bridge became very quiet.

Eight hours have passed since the Aon starship left the bloated star far behind. On the bridge, Captain York remarks to the Aon ladies and First Officer Simpson, "That was quite a sight, seeing a star, firsthand, going nova."

"Yes, and those sights are quite rare," said Atheasis.

"What's even rarer than that," remarked Russ, "is a super-nova."

Conversation ended abruptly, as the scanners indicate a large fleet of ships just ahead.

“There must be thousands of vessels,” exclaimed Trais, “but they are traveling way below light speed.”

“Just how fast are they going?” asked Dick.

“They are going at about a thousand miles a second,” responded Trais.

“What kind of propulsion system are they using?” asked Russ.

“They are powered by an ion propulsion system,” answered Trais.

“They sure are using an ancient system,” said Barthena. “We quit using that thousands of years ago.”

“There is something else that the scanners show,” said Trais, “the beings aboard are frozen and in metal crypts.”

“Well, that sure brings back old memories of when we used the cryogenics method to enable us to embark on star travel,” said Dick.

“Yes, it sure does and quite fond memories, by the way,” mused Russ.

"One thing I feel sure of," said Dick, "is that they came from that burning out star we passed just hours ago."

"The star was probably in the process of burning out for hundreds of years," said Russ.

"I sure hope they find a new home," said Barthena.

Everyone on board agreed with this wish. In a short time the fleet of ships was left far behind, as the Aon ship headed for the next star. Five more days go by, and the ship is again near a star. As they slow, they are able to detect five planets revolving around this star.

"Our scanners show that we have just gone through a cloud of insects, and literally, trillions of them have collected on the ship," reports Trais.

"That is very strange," remarks Atheasis. "This is the first time our ship has run into any insects in interstellar space."

"Are they alive?" asked Barthena.

"Yes, very much so," said Trais. A look of fright suddenly appears on Trais' face and she cries, "Oh no! No! It can't be."

"What's the matter?" asked Atheasis.

"The insects are now eating through the outer wall of the ship," reported Trais.

"How long will it take them to eat through the wall?" asked Atheasis, in a shaking, frightened voice.

"If they continue at the rate they are going now, they will eat through in thirty minutes (Trais quotes a time period, which would be equal to thirty minutes in Earth time)," said Trais. "What shall we do?"

"Let's increase our speed and do some quick turns to see if that will knock them off," said Atheasis.

Trais agreed. In a short time, she reported that all the violent maneuvers had had no effect on the insects.

"We've just got to destroy them before they get to the inner wall of the ship, for if they get through to the inside, we are doomed," said Atheasis.

"I wonder how the atmosphere of one of these planets would affect them?"

"I don't know whether it would kill them or not, but it's certainly worth a try," said Trais.

"All right, let's head into the atmosphere of the outermost planet," said Atheasis.

"Okay, but we'd better hurry, as they've already eaten through the outer wall," reports Trais.

"Very well, let's go full power to our photon drive engines. That's the fastest we dare go, or we will overshoot the planet. Just before we enter the planet's atmosphere, we'll convert to anti-magnetic power," said Atheasis.

"Fine," said Trais.

"They've already demonstrated how well they can survive in space," said Barthena. "Let's hope that the planet's atmosphere proves to be their downfall."

The other two Aon women shared Barthena's wish. As they came ever nearer to the outer planet, the insects were still eating feverishly away at the ship.

"They are eating our equipment on their way to the inside," said Trais. "If this planet's atmosphere doesn't kill them, we won't have time to reach another planet before our ship is completely destroyed. All we can do now, is to pray that Zith will bring us through safely."

The ship has now been converted to anti-magnetic power as the planet looms ahead. Shortly, they enter the planet's atmosphere, which Trais reports is at 1200 degrees. The ship is leveled off so that it skims over the planet's surface.

"The insects are now eating slower, but they still survive," reports Trais.

"How tough they are that they can stand this hostile environment," exclaims Barthena.

"They have quit eating on our ship and are now slowly dying," exclaimed Trais with glee.

With this news, there was great jubilation and cheers on the bridge.

"They are now dying more quickly and falling off the ship in big bunches," said Trais.

"Okay, let's continue through this atmosphere until we are positive that every last insect is dead," said Atheasis.

"All right," answered Trais.

In just minutes, Trais reported that every insect was now dead.

"Okay, give full power to the anti-magnetic engines. We're leaving this planet," said Atheasis.

Trais and Barthena quickly responded to Atheasis' orders and they were soon out in the blackness of space again.

"Trais, I want you to remain at full power on our anti-magnetic engines, and I want you and Barthena to do a complete check on the condition of the ship and report back to me immediately," ordered Atheasis.

Trais and Barthena immediately turned to start their tests.

"Oh, one more thing before you start. I think we should also call in our staff of engineers," said Atheasis.

"That sounds like a good idea," agreed Trais.

Then she and Barthena started to work on the problem. About an hour later, they reported to Atheasis that the ship was in critical condition.

"We have lost our main engine—the stored cloud power engine," said Trais.

“How are the other two engines?” asked Atheasis.

“They are all right, but what really worries me is the fact that the insects have done severe damage to our life-support system,” said Trais.

“Can it be repaired?” asked Atheasis.

“Yes, we have enough material in the storage area to take care of the repairs, but what makes it so critical is the fact that we’re racing against time. If we don’t get it repaired in time, we will all be doomed,” said Trais with a deeply worried look on her face.

“Okay, get every available man and woman to work on it and let’s get started right now,” said Atheasis.

Trais and Barthena left hurriedly to get every available person to work on this matter of life and death.

Chapter XXVI THE ANGELS

The crippled Aon starship now heads out of this solar system and on to the next star. They have switched to full photon drive power. Now that they do not have the use of the stored cloud power engines, stars that would have been hours or maybe days away, are now years away. Luckily, the insects' damage to the ship was confined to the lower decks. None of the upper decks were damaged at all. At the bridge, Atheasis asks Trais how the repairs are coming along.

"Well, right now, it looks very good. I feel confident that we will get the life-support system repaired in time," said Trais.

"That's the best news I've heard yet," said Atheasis. "How about the stored cloud power engines?"

"Well, to be honest with you, we have concentrated our efforts on the life-support system, and have done very little about the stored cloud power engines," answered Trais.

"I can understand that the life-support system was of top priority," said Atheasis.

"As it stands now, the life support system repairs are coming along so well that in a short while, we'll be able to devote all our time to the stored cloud power engine," said Trais. "Of course, I'm sure you already realize that even after we get this engine fixed, we will still have to resort to our photon drive engines. We have lost all of the stored energy and won't be able to replace it until we go through some more interstellar space gas clouds again.

"Well, I guess I'd better get back to work on the repairs," she continued.

"That sounds good," said Atheasis.

Several hours later, the Aons, with help from the Earthlings, have completed repairs on the life-support system and the stored cloud power engine. In Captain York's apartment on the ship's apartment deck, York, Simpson, and Harrison are visiting.

"I've certainly got to hand it to the Aon women. They know how to run a ship," said York. The other two men were in complete agreement.

"I think the way they have been able to handle critical situations has been utterly fantastic," said Simpson.

"I think they would be an outstanding crew on anybody's ship," Harrison added.

"Yes, they certainly would," agreed Dick, "and I've got some good news to report. I was just down at the bridge, and Atheasis tells me that their instruments indicate that there are some more interstellar space gas clouds about three light weeks away."

"Wow, that is good news," exclaimed Russ.

"I can't wait until we're back to that tremendous speed of 1500 times the speed of light," said Jack.

Several days later, York and Virena are talking as they stroll through the parks on the recreation deck. Virena says, "I have been hearing voices that claim to be the Angels of God and say that we must go back! Go back! They say that we have gone too far and are now in the forbidden zone."

"That is very interesting," said York. "I wonder what it means."

"I have been very perplexed by it, because I feel that there is something more to it, but I can't seem to pick up anything more on it. I have never had a problem like this before," said Virena.

"Have you discussed it with anybody else?" asked York.

"Yes, I have and I find that all of the other Aon women also received a message. They, too, haven't been able to pick up any more information," said Virena.

"This is all very strange. I can't understand it," said York.

"Well, you're not alone. I feel the same way," said Virena as they parted.

Days and weeks went by, seemingly very slowly, but the ship was still traveling at light speed. They soon reached the vicinity of the first interstellar space cloud they had encountered for some time. They discovered that there were five such clouds. Passing through them, the ship's speed increased ten times and on up to 1500 times light speed. York, on the bridge with the Aon women, asked why the speed of the ship stayed the same from the fourth to the fifth cloud instead of increasing.

"It didn't increase speed going through the last cloud, because that is the maximum speed we can achieve," answered Atheasis.

"Well, that is still plenty fast," said York. "I never dreamed I would ever travel that fast until I came aboard this ship. It still blows my mind."

"We have gotten pretty used to these speeds through the years," said Atheasis.

"Of course, for a long time light speed was as fast as our ships could go. We just recently discovered the secret of power in the interstellar space gas clouds," added Trais.

"Yes, it was certainly a big breakthrough for us," said Barthena.

Changing the subject, York asked, "Have you ladies still been experiencing the voices from the Angels?"

"Yes, we have, and it is even intensifying," said Atheasis.

"This is very interesting. I hope we can find an answer to the phenomenon," said York.

"So do we," exclaimed Atheasis.

"Have you received any more information about it?" asked York.

"No, we haven't. We don't know any more than we did before," answered Atheasis. Dick then decided to leave the bridge and let the girls get back to work.

Several more days pass as the Aon starship continues on at 1/6 of a light year an hour. On the bridge, the women see four vessels flash past the ship as if it were standing still.

"I can't believe that they went by us as if we weren't moving," said Trais.

"Well, we've finally come upon ships that are a lot faster than ours," said Atheasis.

"I guess it was bound to happen sooner or later. We have the fastest ships in our galaxy, and we've criss-crossed over half of this one before we met our match," said Barthena.

"I always felt that we would run into ships that were faster than ours someday," said Atheasis.

"It kind of scares me," said Barthena. "What if they're unfriendly? We won't be able to escape them."

"All we can do now is to hope and pray that they are friendly," said Atheasis.

"It could be that they have other plans than to bother with us," said Trais.

"Let's hope so," remarked Atheasis. "Have they shown any indication of slowing down to check us out more thoroughly?"

"No," answered Trais.

"Wow! I would like to know how fast they are going and what kind of propulsion system they use," cried York.

Trais said, "I am completely unfamiliar with their propulsion system, but as to their speed, my scanners and sensors show that they are traveling at one light year an hour."

"Wow! A light year an hour. That's awfully fast. I had been wondering if we would ever run into a ship faster than ours," said York. "I guess we have now."

Silence settled over the bridge with only the pulsating sound of the scanners to break the quiet.

Suddenly Trais exclaimed, "The scanners show that the alien ships have slowed down."

"At what speed are they?" asked Atheasis.

"They are down to our speed now and even slower," answered Trais. "In fact, they are turning around and heading toward us."

At this news, the atmosphere became very tense. Everyone on the bridge wondered if the strange vessels were coming back to attack them. If this were the fact, those on the Aon ship were, indeed, helpless, as they had very few weapons and they would be unable to outrun their attackers as they had so many times before.

Everyone on the bridge was praying that the alien ships meant no harm. However, shortly they came alongside the Aon ship and went into formation around it, with one in front, one behind, and one on either side. They were triangular in shape. They were pacing the Aon ship now and continued to do so for about thirty minutes, then they took off, leaving the Aon ship quickly behind.

"Why, they make us look absolutely ridiculous," exclaimed Atheasis.

In a short time Trais reported that the vessels were slowing down. Within an hour, they were well below the Aons' speed. Then soon, they pulled alongside the Aon starship again, and immediately, the image of a beautiful female came on the Aon ship's screen. The Earthlings who witnessed the vision agreed that she equaled in beauty, the lovely Aon women.

Dressed in a silvery uniform, she started to speak, "I am Corlena, head of the Angels of God. You are now in the forbidden zone, and I must ask that you either turn back or settle on our planet."

Atheasis answered, "I am Atheasis, captain and commander of this starship. We come in peace and mean no harm to anyone."

"Why then, have you invaded our area?" asked Corlena.

"We have been searching for a livable planet ever since we were driven off the planet, Aon, by a warlike race called Aldans," said Atheasis.

"I would like to board your ship and discuss your problem further," said Corlena.

"Fine," said Atheasis, "I will prepare the ship so that you can board."

"That will not be necessary. We can board your ship without any preparation on your part," said Corlena.

Three small clouds then appeared on the Aon bridge. The clouds faded and there stood Corlena and two other female Angels, all dressed in silvery clothing.

"How in the world did you do that? Did you used some kind of transporting machine to arrive on this ship?" asked York.

"No, we have complete control of the molecules in our bodies," explained Corlena.

"You mean you did it with mind control?" asked the surprised York.

"I guess you could put it that way," said Corlena.

"With powers like that, you must be either angels of God, or Gods, yourselves," said Dick.

The Earthlings were all in agreement with York, but the Aons were still skeptical.

"With me are Dithesa and Olana," said Corlena.

"We are very pleased to meet you," said Atheasis.

"We are also very happy to meet all of you, too," said Corlena. "However, if you should choose to go beyond our planet, we will have to destroy your ship, and we don't want to do that."

"Well, we can't go back, and since we have been looking for so long for a planet on which we can live, we accept your invitation to settle on yours," said Atheasis.

"All right, I will then guide you to our sun and to the one and only planet, Cercin, orbiting that sun," said Corlena. "I will have my ships escort you."

"Fine," said Atheasis. "Would you like a tour of our ship?"

"We would like that very much," answered Corlena.

As they toured the ship, Atheasis remarked, "I'll have to say that you have the most fantastic ships I have ever seen. Are they the fastest in your galaxy?"

"They are not only the fastest in our galaxy, but also, the fastest in the universe," replied Corlena.

"That, I can believe, because we have the fastest ship in our galaxy and yours made ours seem ridiculous," said Atheasis. "What kind of propulsion system do you use? We are completely unfamiliar with it."

"We use the coragon-drive," replied Corlena.

"What is that?" asked Atheasis.

"We have underground rocks on our planet from which we can develop tremendous power. They are called coragon rocks and are found only on our planet," explained Corlena.

"How very interesting," remarked Atheasis as they continued the tour of the ship. After showing Corlena all the decks of the ship, the women returned to the bridge.

Several hours later, the travelers approached the Angels' star and single planet. Atheasis gave the order to slow down, and shortly the Cercin planet appeared as a small globe. They slow down even further.

"I think you will find our planet to be very beautiful," said Dithesa. "We have many lovely gardens all over our planet."

"I am sure we will find it to be very lovely," answered Atheasis.

"Do you see that asteroid over there in the distance?" asked Olana, pointing out the window of the ship.

Everyone on the bridge indicated that they did indeed, see it. Then, Corlena, Dithesa and Olana pressed their fingers to their foreheads, in extreme concentration as their eyes turned all white. The Earthlings and Aons continued watching the asteroid when, suddenly, it blew up into thousands of pieces. Minutes later, though, the pieces came back together, looking exactly as it had before exploding. This latest feat of mind control by the Angels thoroughly convinced the Earthlings that they must indeed, be Angels of God, but the Aons were still more skeptical.

Soon, following more lessening of speed, both the Aon and the Angel ships entered the atmosphere of Cercin. They found themselves over a city. Soon, they landed in a large area behind the Angels' palace. All the Angels and the total of 563 passengers aboard the Aon ship disembarked and started walking toward Corlena's palace, passing beautiful gardens with exotic plants and flowers of every color. York commented on the beauty of the gardens, comparing them to the Garden of Eden back on Earth. The plants were different from anything the Earthlings or the Aons had ever seen.

"Do you have the power to live forever?" asked Atheasis.

"Yes, we do," answered Corlena.

"Do you use a rejuvenation machine to achieve immortality?" asked Trais.

"No," replied Corlena, "we know what's going on with our bodies so well that we can, with our minds, repair any organ or tissues that may deteriorate."

"How very interesting," said Barthena.

The Earth people listened in awe to the story told by the Angels. Soon the group arrived at and entered the palace.

When they were inside the palace, Corlena asked if they would like something to eat or drink.

"That would be very nice," said Atheasis.

They walked through the palace until they came to a huge hall with tables and chairs set up. The group was seated with the Earthlings seated with Aons and Angels. Although the food was different than any that either the Earth or Aon people had ever tasted, they all enjoyed it very much and agreed that it was delicious. Corlena asked if everyone had had enough to eat. The Earthlings and Aons answered affirmatively and said that it was really delicious.

Corlena remarked, "I'm glad that you have had plenty to eat, because you are going to need plenty of food in your bodies to be ready for the good hard work you will be doing."

"What are you talking about?" asked York.

"I am referring to the work you will all be doing in our coragon mines," answered Corlena.

"It might very well be that we would be willing to work in your mines, but first I think we should have an agreement as to the compensation and working conditions," said York.

"You will not receive any compensation, nor will we make any agreement with you," said Corlena.

"What?" exclaimed Queen Virena. "Do you mean to say that you expect us to work in your mines as slaves? No way!"

"I think you will," replied Corlena.

At that moment, two Angel guards came into the room and Corlena instructed them to change Virena's mind. The guards put their fingers to their foreheads and their eyes turned a pure white. Virena cried out in pain. She fell to the floor and the pain seemed to grow worse. The pain finally got so bad that she curled into the fetal position and begged Corlena to stop.

"Are you ready to work in our mines?" asked Corlena.

"Yes, yes! I will!" cried Virena.

"Good," said Corlena, "and if the rest of you Aons and Earth people give us any trouble, we will make you very sorry. Now, all of you will follow these six guards to the mines."

With that, the Earthlings and Aons arose from their chairs and followed the guards. They were led down stairways to an underground, dimly lit passageway. They soon arrived at the digging area, where they were given instruments with which to dig and told to get to work immediately.

Hours passed and as the Earthlings and Aons continue to work, they noticed a very old man who looked exhausted from the many hours of continuous work and who had slowed down considerably. A guard also had noticed the old man and, as before, his eyes turned all white and the old man fell to the ground in pain.

A few minutes later, the guard's eyes had returned to normal and he said, "Okay, old man, now get back to work and a lot faster than you were or you're going before Queen Corlena."

"I will! I will! But please don't take me to the drainage machine," pleaded the old man.

Captain York and the other new workers wondered just what the drainage machine was, which the old man feared so much.

More hours slipped by and the Earthlings, Aons, and all the others, who were allowed very little sleep and food, heard the guard abusing the old man again.

"What is this? I thought I told you to speed up your work and here you have slowed down again, old man," said the Cercin guard. "You're going before Queen Corlena right now."

"Oh no! Please, I don't want to go to the drainage machine," begged the old man.

"All I know is that you are going before Queen Corlena, and whatever she decides to do with you is up to her," said the guard.

The old man was escorted to the throne room, where Queen Corlena was seated on her throne.

"Your Majesty, I have brought before you this old man who has been continually disobedient and slow at his work," said the guard.

"Good, I'm glad you have brought him," said Corlena. "What have you to say for yourself, old man?"

"I have been slow in my work, but I couldn't help it, as I was completely exhausted. I just couldn't go any faster," explained the old man.

"Whether you were tired or not, does not matter to me. What does matter is that you were cutting down production and this, I will not tolerate," said Corlena and then to the guard, "Now, I want you to lock him up in our dungeon."

"All right, Your Majesty," said the guard and with that, he escorted the old man out of the throne room and to the dungeon.

There was great excitement at the mines the next day, when a vein of coragon rocks was uncovered. The find was tremendous, figuring into the millions of tons. The coragon rocks were green in color and gave off a weird glow. All of the workers were immediately put to work loading the rocks into carts to be taken to various storage areas. They would later be used in Cercin starships. One coragon rock about the size of a human fist would give the ship enough power to run for weeks at a speed of one light year an hour.

Two days later, guards stopped work in the mines and took the workers to Queen Corlena's courtroom. They were told to sit down. Queen Corlena, with three guards on either side of her, sat in front of them.

She soon stood up and said, "I have had you people brought before me to show you what happens to those who disobey me or my guards. Over to my right, you have probably noticed a cabinet with a see-through front. This is the drainage machine. In case there are any of you who are not familiar with this machine, I shall tell you about it. It gets its name from the fact that it will drain every drop of water out of a living body. I have sent guards down to bring a very disobedient mine worker before you."

Corlena then sat down. Soon, the guards brought the old man in.

"Okay, put that no-good worker into the drainage machine," ordered Corlena.

The guards brought the screaming, kicking old man up to the machine, opened the door, threw him in, and closed and locked the door. The switches were thrown on. Lights of all colors flashed and there was a whirring sound. Soon, there were terrible screams of agony from the machine, which rose above the machine's noise. The old man pounded on the glass door, begging to be let out. In less than an hour his body took on a grotesque appearance. Many of the watchers started to vomit. Tears could be seen in the eyes of others.

"I would like to go right up there and choke Corlena until she fell to the floor dead," exclaimed York.

Russ felt the same way, but they both knew that because of the super powers of the Cercins, they were powerless to do anything. Corlena's horror show continued for another hour, when the machine was shut off. The onlookers saw all that was left of the old man—an indistinguishable pile of debris lying at the bottom of the horrible torture machine.

Corlena then started to speak again, "You have just seen a sample of what can happen to anyone of you that are slow, insolent, or disobedient. Now, get back to work and you'd better start working a lot harder than you have been."

After hearing the evil queen, everyone filed out with the horrible image still on their minds. Some became terribly sick. Others just cried sorrowfully as they left the room.

The next day the miners extracted many tons of coragon rocks. Suddenly, something strange seemed to have happened to the queen's guards. They became still and looked like statues. York and Simpson quit their work and walked over to the guards.

"What do you make of it, Dick?" asked Russ.

"I don't know, but it looks to me as if all the guards in the mine have been put into a state of suspended animation," said Dick. He touched one of the guards, but there was no sign of movement from him.

Not only the Earthlings, but also all the Aons and other workers came over to view this strange phenomenon.

"Shall we go up to the main floor?" asked Dick.

"We may as well," answered Atheasis.

So the workers, of all races, rushed out of the mine and up to the main floor, where they found the same conditions as they had seen in the mine. The guards and all of Queen Corlena's court were frozen into strange positions, sitting, standing, or whatever. The workers went on into the throne room where they found Corlena in the same trancelike state, sitting on her throne.

Captain York shook his head and asked, "What do you make of it?"

"I don't know. It's got me puzzled, too," said Atheasis. "Maybe we can search around and find some clue as to what happened."

"That sounds like a good idea," agreed Dick.

Chapter XXVII RESCUED

"What I can't understand is why we and all the other mine workers weren't thrown into this state of suspended animation, as the Cercins were," wondered Russ.

"I sure can't answer that, Russ. All I know is that whatever it was, only the Cercins were susceptible for some mysterious reason," said Dick.

The group which was still mobile, decided to go outside to look around. They found the Cercins outside to be in the same trancelike, immobile condition as those inside. While they were looking at the Cercins, they saw a strange looking spaceship descending from the sky. As it came closer, they could see that it was going to land to the back of the palace. Upon landing, a door of the ship opened and steps appeared.

Little men came out of the ship, descended the stairs and stepped onto the ground. The spectators could then see that the beings were only four or five feet tall, with a whiter skin than any they had ever seen. They had very large eyes that seemed to extend around to the sides of their heads. They had a slit for a mouth and no nose. They all wore black uniforms. There were about a dozen men who came out of the ship and they dispersed to all directions.

One of them headed for the group of Earthlings and Aons, and started to speak, "I am Kaylon, leader of the Pararines race. We have come to rescue all the captives in the Cercin mines."

"Was it you guys who were responsible for the Cercins being thrown into a state of suspended animation?" asked York.

"Yes, we used our mind control to do it," said Kaylon. "We thought we would never be able to break through their defenses, as they were such a powerful race, but we finally discovered a weakness and broke through."

"How long can you hold them in this state?" asked Atheasis.

"About two Earth days. That should give you enough of a head start to make your escape," answered Kaylon.

"Yes, that should give us enough time," agreed Atheasis.

"Whether we can hold them long enough to be tried for their crimes is another matter," said Kaylon. "One drawback for us is the fact that although we can go at 5000 times the speed of light in our ships, the Cercins are capable of going almost twice as fast."

"What kind of power source do your ships used?" asked York, with curiosity.

"Our primary engines used black holes for power," said Kaylon.

"Gee, that's interesting," said York.

"I sure hope you are able to hold the Cercins for trial," said Russ.

"We sure hope we can, too," said Kaylon. "They have caused havoc in our galaxy for many years and their reputation for torture and cruelty is well known. We want to put an end to Queen Corlena and her evil slave trade."

"We can sure testify as to the cruelty of Corlena and the Cercins," said York.

"You'd better not waste any more time," said Kaylon. "You'd better get out of here right now."

Atheasis agreed, and she and her crew and passengers quickly left Kaylon and rushed toward their ship, after expressing their gratitude to him and the Pararines.

Shortly, the Aons and Earthlings were aboard, and Atheasis gave the order for full power to the anti-magnetic engines, and they soon left the Cercin planet far behind and were shortly on full photon-drive power.

Hours pass and there is a heated discussion going on between York, Simpson, and Harrison in York's apartment on the second deck.

"You know, it is really something, the life forms and powerful and super-advanced civilizations we have come across," said Russ.

"Yes, it is, but when I think back to the Cercins, it saddens me," mused Dick.

"Why does it sadden you?" asked Jack.

"Well, they were of such an advanced culture and could have done so much real good for their galaxy. Instead they turned to evil," replied Dick.

The other men agreed with Dick and the unpleasant subject was dropped.

"I was just down at the bridge and Atheasis said that we have come to a big gap in the galaxy, where there are no stars for the next 200 parsecs," said Dick.

"Wow! That's quite a gap, alright," said Jack.

"I guess we can stand that," said Russ, "but, it might start getting boring not reaching any stars for months."

"There's more to it than that," said Dick, "Atheasis told me that the scanners have detected a tremendous amount of matter in this area."

"Will we be in any danger of colliding with this material?" asked Russ.

"No, she assured me we wouldn't," replied Dick, "However, she said that there seems to be some fluid along with the matter, and she feels that with the tremendous mass of matter and fluid, it could slow the starship down considerably."

"Would it destroy the ship?" asked Jack.

"No, she felt sure that wouldn't happen," said Dick.

"I find this fluid in space very interesting. Is it a water-like fluid?" Russ asked.

"No, Atheasis tells me that it is like nothing they have ever experienced," said Dick. "I might also add, it's like nothing I have ever seen either, according to her description."

"So, we can go through it safely, but it will slow us down. Is that about what it boils down to?" asked Russ.

"That's right," answered Dick.

"Did you find out how much it will slow us?" asked Jack.

"Well, they haven't completely analyzed the data from the computers and scanners yet, but they should soon know," said Dick.

"I sure hope it isn't too much," said Russ.

"Atheasis thought, off the top of her head, that it might slow down to about light speed," said Dick.

"Wow, that is quite a reduction," said Russ. "Of course, once we get through the area, we will immediately, start to gain speed again," Dick said.

"Well, that's good news," said Jack.

"Do you know what this area makes me think of?" asked Russ.

"No, what?" asked Dick.

"This area seems to me to be a sort of interstellar space sludge," said Russ.

"Well, I guess you're right," said Dick, as Jack and Russ left to return to their own apartments.

Two more days passed and the Aon starship finally arrived at the area, which Russ had described as interstellar space sludge. When the ship enters this area, it immediately starts to slow down, dropping quickly from 1500 times light speed to 1499.

Back on deck two at Captain York's apartment, the three men, Dick, Jack and Russ are reminiscing of days gone by.

"I was just thinking of the good old days of the Triton," said Dick.

"Yes, those were quite the days, all right," said Simpson.

"It was kind of scary for a while, when we learned that our sun was going nova," said Harrison.

"Yes, it sure was scary," said York, "but, I'll never forget that good old ship, because if it wasn't for her, we wouldn't be alive today."

"She certainly was quite a ship," agreed Simpson.

"The thing that really amazes me," said York, "is the fact that before we were forced to find another planet by circumstances beyond our control, I had never thought of traveling like this, not even to the nearest star to Earth."

"Yeah, I felt the same way," said Simpson, "especially when you realize that the nearest star to Earth, Proxima Centauri, was 4.2 light years or 25,000,000,000,000 miles, and traveling at 3,600,000 miles an hour, it was still a trip of 792 years."

"Of course, we all knew that the Triton was not considered capable of such star travel, but we had no choice," said Harrison.

"Well, even if our chances were only one in a million or even one in a billion, it was better than no chance at all," commented York.

"It was really a miracle to think that we made it, when thousands of the starships which left Earth did not survive," said Simpson.

"Yes, it was certainly the gamble of all time, but I'm sure we all agree that it was well worth the risk," said York.

"I can never forget, though, that we could never have made it if the technique of body freezing had not been developed," said Harrison.

"That's right, it was the whole key to our success," said York.

Two more days passed, and the Aon starship now slowed to 1000 times light speed. York remarks to Simpson, who is visiting him in his apartment, "According to Barthena, we're coming to the edge of the galaxy."

"Isn't that something? Here we have criss-crossed another galaxy without finding a planet on which we can live," said Simpson.

"Of course, we don't have to worry since we have access to the rejuvenating machine, but it is still discouraging. We have all the pleasures and comforts of this great ship, but one finally gets a feeling of being cooped up anyway," said Dick.

"That's right," agreed Russ.

"I guess when we reach that outer edge of stars and still haven't found a planet, we'll just double back and keep going back and forth through this galaxy until we do, hopefully, find a planet," said Dick.

"Yes, we'll just have to be patient, I guess," said Russ.

"We've already encountered so many strange worlds and life forms, and such super-advanced societies, that I wonder what we'll run into next," wondered Dick.

"Isn't this sludge something?" said Russ. "I wonder how much more we'll be slowed before we get through it. Have you talked to the Aon ladies on the bridge anymore?"

"No, I haven't had any more information since Atheasis' prediction that we would be slowed to light speed," said Dick.

"Well, I guess we'll soon know for sure," said Russ. "Well, I'd better get back to my apartment."

After several weeks, the Aon starship was finally through the space sludge, after being slowed to a minimum of twice light speed. They then started gaining speed again.

Chapter XXVIII SUPER BEING

The Aon ship returned to its maximum speed of over a trillion miles an hour and left the space sludge far behind. York was on the bridge visiting with the Aon ladies as they neared the first star since leaving the sludge area. As they draw nearer to the star, they can see that there are four planets revolving around it.

Atheasis gives the order to slow down and they soon go into orbit around the first planet, but the scanners and sensors indicate that it is a very dead planet. They quickly leave and head for the next planet. They reach the second planet and go into a 500-mile high orbit over the planet. Trais started reporting immediately to Atheasis about the conditions on the planet.

"It is indicated that the atmosphere is breathable for Aons and Earthlings alike," she said. "The planet is also rich enough in vegetation to be life supporting."

"That is very good news," said Atheasis.

There was great joy on the bridge when the news was announced.

"Is there any animal life?" asked Atheasis.

"Yes, there is. In fact, there seems to be some very primitive beings there," answered Trais. "They seem to be riding on these strange animals, which seems to be their only mode of travel."

Trais reported that these people seemed to have very little in the way of machinery, and their cities appear to be very primitive.

"It is my opinion that we should not land here, for to do so might cause a cultural shock to them," said Trais.

"I agree with you," said Atheasis, and she gave the order to go out of orbit and head for the next planet.

York said, “The way you described those people and their planet, it sounds like the Earth back in the 19th century. It would even be primitive by our standards now, too.”

The ship soon reached the next planet, which proved to be lifeless, so they continued on to the next one, which also, proved lifeless. After checking out the whole solar system, which their equipment indicated was unfriendly to life, Atheasis was forced to give the order to leave the system.

Thirty hours later, on deck one, at the bridge, Trais reports that the scanners and sensors have picked up a vessel approaching them.

“Is it a warship?” asked Atheasis.

Trais indicated that she wasn’t able to tell yet, as the vessel was too far away.

“Well, keep me posted of any further developments,” said Atheasis.

“I surely will,” answered Trais.

The Aon ship continues on at 1500 times the speed of light, when Trais reported that the strange vessel was on a course heading directly for the Aon ship.

A few minutes later, Trais said, "The scanners and sensors now show that there are some weapons aboard the ship, but I still don't know whether it is a warship or whether they mean any harm to us."

The ship then came alongside the Aon ship and an image appeared on their screen. He seemed to be a giant, possibly over ten feet tall, with greyish-colored skin, bulging eyes, dome-shaped forehead, two holes for a nose, and a slit for a mouth.

He spoke, "I am Dalith, one of many who patrol this area of the galaxy."

Atheasis introduced herself as captain of the Aon starship.

"I am glad to meet you, and I mean no harm to your ship or any of its passengers," said the giant. "I have come to give you a grave warning."

"What is it you wish to warn us about?" asked Atheasis.

The giant continued, "You will soon be coming to an area where a great war is being waged among numerous solar systems. This area spans half a dozen parsecs in every direction. If you don't wish to be involved in this, you must turn back, or if you desire, I can give you directions for an alternate route, so that you can continue your journey."

"I surely want to thank you for the warning, and we would like directions for missing that area," replied Atheasis.

"Okay, could I talk with your navigator, then?" asked Dalith.

Atheasis quickly called Barthena, and Dalith gave the navigational coordinates to her, after which he and his ship sped away on a different route than the one on which they had approached.

Hours slipped into weeks as the Aon starship continued on at its maximum speed of over a trillion miles an hour. They have now gone beyond the area where the great war was being waged. At the bridge on Deck one, Atheasis has given the order to slow down as they near another star. As they draw closer, they discover that there is only one planet revolving around the star.

As they slow down even more, Trais said, “I am receiving very strong signals from that planet.”

“Are they signals of an intelligent race trying to contact us?” asked Atheasis.

“We are still too far away to tell,” replied Trais.

As they got closer to the planet, while traveling on anti-magnetic power, the planet appears as a small globe to all on the Aon ship.

“The signals are getting stronger now and I can definitely tell you that the signals are coming from an intelligent race on the planet,” said Trais.

They are soon into an 850-mile-high orbit over the planet, and there is tremendous excitement as all those on board are wondering and hoping that this is a life-supporting planet upon which they can settle. As they continue to orbit the planet, more information is being received from the scanners and sensors.

“Why, it’s unbelievable! I can’t believe it,” said Trais.

“What’s the matter?” asked Atheasis.

"Those signals we are receiving are not coming from a whole race of beings, but from only one, and the signals are getting stronger," reported Trais.

"Why, that's impossible," said Atheasis, "signals that strong couldn't come from just one individual. You'd better double check your readouts."

I have double checked and it definitely shows that the signals are coming from only one being on the planet and all of the signals are from the being's thought processes alone," insisted Trais.

"For a being to transmit such powerful signals as these is absolutely fantastic. He certainly has super power," said Atheasis.

"I will certainly agree with that," said Trais. "According to my scanner and sensor readouts, if we were down on the planet's surface face to face with this super being, we would not be able to survive the tremendous energy generated from his massive brain. It would surely kill us. Of course, he wouldn't mean to harm us. It's just that his brain is so massive compared to ours."

"Do you think we will be safe from him while orbiting around the planet?" asked Atheasis.

"No, I don't. The energy from his brain has now become so powerful that I think if we stay in orbit much longer, it might destroy our ship," answered Trais.

Upon hearing Trais' predictions, Atheasis immediately gave the order to leave the orbit at once. Full power was given to the anti-magnetic engines, and the ship was soon up to 10,000,000 miles an hour. There is terror on all the faces on the bridge, as the signals from the planet become ever more powerful.

Atheasis orders the switch to full photon-drive power, which takes them up to the speed of light.

"Have the signals gotten any weaker?" asked Atheasis.

"They have weakened a little, but not much," said Trais. "I don't know if we can get far enough away before he destroys us."

Then Atheasis ordered full power to the stored cloud power engines, and they are soon back up to 1500 times light speed.

"How are the signals coming in, now?" asked Atheasis.

"They are weakening some but are still awfully strong. I don't . . . . . ." Trais answer broke off, and she stood like a statue, as did everyone else on the ship. All were frozen into whatever position they were in at the moment, as they were all thrown into a state of suspended animation.

Chapter XXIX BEYOND THE GALAXIES

It has been 6,689,689 Earth years since all of the crew and passengers were thrown into suspended animation by the super being, and the Aon starship is now ten billion light years beyond Proxima Centauri. On the bridge, the crew is starting to come back to life. Trais is the first to come back to normal. She shakes her head trying to get a grasp on what has happened. She asked Atheasis what happened.

"I don't know," answered Atheasis, "but let's find out."

"All right, I'll check the memory banks, scanners and sensor readouts," said Trais.

"I'll check the navigational coordinates," said Barthena.

As Trais and Barthena are gathering all of the information for their captain, York and Simpson arrive on the scene. "What in the world has happened here? I feel like I have just come out of a deep sleep," said York.

"Well, that's about what happened," answered Trais.

"Yes, but just exactly what did happen? I feel so strange," said Simpson.

"Well, as far as we can tell, we were put into suspended animation by some super being on the last planet we orbited," replied Trais.

"How long were we in that condition and where are we now?" asked Dick.

"According to the information we have right now, we have been in suspended animation for 6,689,689 Earth years, and we are ten billion light years beyond Proxima Centauri," said Trais.

Captain York and First Officer Simpson were dumbfounded at this shocking news. "Why, that means that we're beyond all the galaxies of the universe," said York in surprise.

"That's right," answered Trais. "Why, we're even beyond the quasars, which are the fastest moving stars at the speed of light, and the furthest-out stars—at least, the furthest we know about," marveled Russ.

"Yes, that's true," said Atheasis, and the women turned back to their work.

Atheasis instructed her crew to turn on the scanners and sensors. Shortly, Trais excitedly announces, "Our sensors and scanners have picked up something really big."

"What is it?" cried Atheasis.

"It seems there's a huge galaxy that all of the billions of the galaxies in our universe orbit around. But, it's kind of misleading to call it a galaxy at all, for it doesn't give off any heat, light, or radiation. It is just a force that holds all of the billions of galaxies in orbit around it," said Trais.

"That is truly fantastic. A super galaxy! I guess that's the only way to explain it. That tremendous force holding all of the galaxies in orbit is amazing," said York.

"So what do we do now? Do we try to escape our universe or try to go back?" asked Russ.

"It would be impossible for us to escape the universe, because of the tremendous mass of the super galaxy and the total mass of all the other galaxies in the universe. It would require a speed beyond what our ship could achieve," answered Trais.

"What velocity would be needed to escape the universe?" York asked.

"It would require a speed of a parsec an hour (3.3 light years an hour)," replied Trais. Atheasis then asked Barthena to figure out the navigational coordinates that would return them to the galaxies.

"This is really something. I thought I would never witness being out beyond the galaxies of our universe, which raises the question I have always had, which is, what is beyond all the galaxies of the universe that we have known? Are there just billions more galaxies, or is there just the blackness of space forever, or is there something I can't even imagine," wondered York.

"Well, it looks like that question will soon be answered," said Russ.

"To answer your questions, according to our scanners and sensors, there are no more stars and galaxies. It looks like there is just the blackness of space forever," said Trais.

After hearing this latest report, York and Simpson returned to their apartments on Deck #2. Several hours later, Barthena had figured out the navigational coordinates, and Atheasis gave the order to head back to the galaxies immediately.

In York's apartment, York and Simpson are talking. "What do you think that super being was, back on that planet? Could it have been God?" asked Russ.

"No, Russ, I don't think it was God even though his brain was so massive that it put us into suspended animation for millions of years," answered Dick.

"If it wasn't God, it was getting real close," remarked Russ.

"Yes, I agree with you," said Dick, "but I think he was just a super-advanced, super-powerful being, but not God. My theory is that throughout the universe there are super-advanced races, and as you sort of go up a ladder, one race after another becomes progressively more advanced until you come to a race that have

God-like powers, and you think of them as Gods, but they aren't. Then you keep going up the ladder of advancement until you reach that most Supreme Being of the universe, and That is God!"

"I wonder what the Aons thought of the super being?" said Russ.

"So far, I haven't had a chance to ask any of them whether they thought the super being on the planet was Zith or not," said Dick.

"Whether they thought it was Zith or not, I feel sure that even they were impressed by the creature's power," insisted Russ.

"Yes, I think you're right, but I'd be willing to bet that they would go along with me that it wasn't God or Zith," said Dick.

"You're probably right," said Russ as he left Dick to return to his own apartment.

Chapter XXX THE PLANET BERENTHIAN

Months passed quickly as the Aon starship continued on at its maximum speed of 1/6 light year an hour. York and Simpson are on the bridge with the Aon women, when Trais said, "The scanners and sensors have picked up an alien vessel at our rear coming at a very fast rate of speed."

"Is it an armed warship?" Atheasis asked.

"No, it is not," answered Trais.

Atheasis asked how many were aboard the vessel.

"There are five crew members, all male," said Trais.

Silence then fell on the bridge with only the yellow flashing lights and the pulsating sound of the scanners breaking the silence. Soon the alien craft pulled alongside the Aon ship. Looking out the ship's windows, the Aons and Earthlings could see that the craft was diamond-shaped, with brightly colored lights encircling it. The ship was a little shorter and narrower than the Aon ship, and it would soon be learned that the ship held friendly people from the planet, Berenthian, the third planet from the star Vorlanthin, which is an outer edge star on an outer galaxy of the universe known by the Aons and Earthlings.

The Berenthian starship was a two-engine ship, its secondary engine using the gravity of stars and planets for its propulsion. With this engine, they could go from hovering to a thousand times the speed of light. The primary engine used black holes as a power source. The energy from a black hole was taken on board ship, where a magnifying machine would magnify this energy so that the maximum speed of the engine would reach a parsec or 3.3 light years an hour.

The image of two Berenthians came on the Aon ship's screen. Except for two features, they looked like Earth people. Their eyes were even more slanted than Oriental Earth people, and they had a horn on top of their heads.

One of them said, "I am Quartin, and this is my First Officer Lasin. We come from the planet Berenthian. We mean no harm to any of you and we would like to come aboard your ship for a visit."

"I am Atheasis, Captain, and we would be pleased to have you come aboard, but first, let us make arrangements so that you may do so," said Atheasis.

"That will not be necessary," said Quartin. "We can board ourselves without special arrangements."

In a short time, two small clouds appeared on the bridge just as the Cercins had previously. The clouds disappeared and revealed Quartin and Lasin, who were dressed in black uniforms with a serpent-like insignia on their chests. They also wore flowing red capes.

"Did you beam aboard our ship with mind control alone?" asked Atheasis.

“Yes. We have complete control over the molecules and atoms in our bodies,” answered Quartin.

“Are you on some kind of mission?” asked Trais.

“No, we were on a sort of pleasure voyage,” answered Quartin.

“Do you have the ability to live forever, and if so, do you do it by mind control or by some kind of machine?” asked Barthena.

“Yes, we can live forever. Our minds keep constantly in tune with our bodies and can repair any bones, organs, or tissue that may deteriorate,” said Quartin.

“Then you have the same powers that the Cercins have,” exclaimed Atheasis.

“Who are the Cercins?” asked Quartin.

“They were a race of people we met very long ago,” said Atheasis.

“Are you on some kind of mission?” asked Lasin.

“No,” answered Atheasis, “we are from the Planet Aon, and we were run out of our solar system by a warlike man and followers.

His name was Zorax. We have been looking for a planet to settle on ever since."

"Oh, how horrible! We have plenty of room on our planet. We have very few guests, and it would be very nice to have you," said Quartin.

"We accept your invitation with pleasure," said Atheasis.

"Wonderful. We will wait impatiently for your arrival," answered Quartin.

The conversation turned to the Berenthian ship. Quartin told the Aons and Earthlings about the propulsion system and the characteristic speed of the two engines.

"Have you escaped our universe?" asked Atheasis. When Quartin answered affirmatively, Trais asked if there was just blackness forever as the Aon sensors and scanners had reported.

"No, there are other universes, the nearest one being 2 ½ trillion light years away" said Quartin.

"Two and a half trillion light years," said Atheasis excitedly. "No wonder we just saw blackness of space. That distance would be beyond the capabilities of our instruments. What kind of universe is it?"

"It's a universe set up just like ours, except that it's an anti-matter universe," answered Quartin.

"And of course, since our universe is a matter universe, we could not enter the other universe, but had to stay a safe distance from it," said Lasin.

"There are also universes of different dimensions and strangely enough, there is a parallel universe that is identical to ours," added Quartin.

"This is absolutely astounding news," said Atheasis.

"Do you have the fastest ships in our universe or in your galaxy?" asked York.

"I don't know about our universe or any of the other universes, but we have the fastest in our galaxy, anyway," answered Quartin.

"Wait now. How about the Tuthian starships?" retorted Lasin.

"Oh come now, you can't be serious. The only reason a Tuthian starship outran us the last time was because I had trouble with my magnifiers. I could beat a Tuthian ship anytime, and even make them look ridiculous," said Quartin disgustedly.

"Now that I think about it, you are right," said Lasin.

As Quartin continued to talk to Atheasis, the Earthlings and Aons noticed that Lasin seemed to be quite nervous.

"What is the matter with you?" asked Quartin, impatiently.

"We've got to get home or we will be late, and don't you remember the last time, when we put a big dent on Dad's starship, he was so mad that he grounded us for a long time," said Lasin.

"Oh, that's right," said Quartin.

Captain York chuckled and whispered to Russ, "Hey, these are just kids out on a joy ride."

"Yeah, isn't it beautiful?" Russ whispered back.

"Hurry up. Let's go," said Lasin.

"Wait, I'm going to give these people the navigational coordinates to find our planet," said Quartin.

"Okay, but hurry up," said Lasin.

Quartin quickly gave the needed information to Barthena and then the two young Berenthians put their fingers to their foreheads in concentration. Their bodies dematerialized into two small clouds, then quickly disappeared. In almost no time, the two Berenthians were back on the ship with their friends. Their ship took off at a high speed. The Aon ship continued on at its trillion mile per hour speed on its way to star system, Vorlanthin-3.

Months go by with a feeling of excitement and hope on the Aon ship, as they all feel that the Berenthians are truly friendly and possibly a religious race of people. They also feel that they have finally found a new home. On Deck #3, Captain York is strolling with his First Officer through one of the ship's beautiful parks.

"One thing I can't get over is the tremendously fast ships that we have encountered," said York.

"They are really amazing, aren't they?" said Russ.

"When we came across the Cercin ships at one light year an hour, I thought that was mighty fantastic, and now we find that the Berenthian ships are capable of triple that speed. It's almost unbelievable," said York.

"When you think about it though, you don't even have to go as far as the Aon, Cercin, or Berenthian starships to be incomprehensible. Most Earthlings couldn't even comprehend the speed of the Triton," said Russ.

"I agree with you there," said York.

"Do you think we will come across any faster ships than the Berenthian's" asked Russ.

"I couldn't even make a guess on that," said York.

"Do you know how many times light speed that parsec an hour that the Berenthians go, figures out to?" asked Russ.

"No, I don't," answered York.

"Well, out of curiosity, I just figured it out," said Russ. "It comes out 29,700 times the speed of light." York just shook his head in amazement.

"Another thing that I find amazing is how advanced their minds are," said Russ. "I feel about as intelligent as a dog or cat in comparison."

"I have that same feeling," added Dick.

"It is really something the way they can repair the bones, organs and tissues of their bodies with mind control alone," said Russ.

"Yes, that is exciting, but the thing I find most fascinating is the way they can beam themselves over to our ship with just mind control," said Dick.

"Can you understand that kind of power?" asked Russ.

"No, not completely, but the idea I have is that they have such complete control over their bodies that they can cause the molecules and atoms in their bodies to line up with the empty spaces between the molecules and atoms of other materials so that they can walk right through it, so to speak," answered York.

"Well, all I can say is that I don't think I'll ever to be able to really understand," said Russ.

"I feel the same way," said Dick, as they started back to their apartments. More months go by before the Aon ship finally nears the star system Vorlanthin 3. Atheasis gave the order to slow the ship as they drew nearer and all aboard were looking out the windows. The ship continues to slow and is now on the anti-magnetic engines. The people at the windows could see that there were nine planets orbiting around the star Vorlanthin. They head for the third planet, which is, of course, the planet Berenthian. Hours slip by and they can see

Berenthian as a small yellow globe. They then go into a 500-mile high orbit around the planet.

The scanners and sensors are turned on and soon indicate that the planet's atmosphere is breathable by Aons and Earth people alike. It is a little thicker than both the Earth's and Aon's planets, but not so much more that they couldn't all adjust to it quite easily. Trais reported that her equipment had picked up on a city on the planet's surface with pyramid-shaped structures.

"They are glass-like but translucent," said Trais. "There is a flashing beacon on one of them."

"Oh, good. That's the signal for us to pinpoint the home of the two brothers, Quartin and Lasin," said Atheasis. "Let's go in for a landing."

"Okay," said Trais, as the big saucer-shaped ship moved ever so slowly closer to the beacon.

They soon landed close to the home of Quartin and Lasin, and all 560 aboard disembarked. As they walked toward the house, they looked up to find that the Berenthian sky was yellow as the planet had appeared from space.

As the group neared the pyramid structure, they were welcomed by the Berenthian brothers, Quartin and Lasin, who told the travelers that they were in the city called Emon. The boys invited the group in to meet their parents. Because there were so many of them, only York, Simpson, Harrison, Benson, Sacks, Queen Virena, Atheasis, Trais, and Barthena went inside. As they came inside, they saw two Berenthian figures dressed in the same black uniforms with red capes and the serpent insignia on their chests, as were worn by Quartin and Lasin. Quartin introduced his mother, Thertrena and his father, Thoranthin.

"We are very glad to meet you both," said Virena.

Quartin and Lasin went outside to talk to the rest of the Aons and Earthlings. The newcomers noticed right away that there was a difference between the boys' mother and father, other than that Thertrena was more feminine. She also had no horn on top of her head as the father and two sons had. They soon learned that this was the distinguishing difference between male and female Berenthians.

"Our sons told us all about you people when they got back from their trip," said Thoranthin.

"We were certainly sorry about the terrible ordeal you have had," said Thertrena.

"There is one thing we can't understand—war. What is it?" asked Thoranthin.

York then explained as best he could what war was.

"Oh, yes," exclaimed Thertrena, "we know what war is, but it has completely gone out of our vocabulary since we haven't had a war in millions of years."

"Well, that is certainly great news to hear," exclaimed Atheasis.

Changing the subject, Thoranthin said, "I have something on my mind that continues to bother me. I wonder if I might be too strict with Quartin and Lasin. I am continually worrying about them, and I am so afraid that they are going to get into some real trouble. I worry that I may be a poor father."

"Oh no, I think you are a very good father. You are just putting some controls on them so that things don't get too far out of hand," said Thertrena, firmly.

"That makes me feel good to hear you say that, and I hope you are right," said Thoranthin.

"Well, I'm sure you're not alone in your doubts," said York. "I think all parents everywhere find it to be very tough to handle their children and be sure they're doing the right thing."

All the Aons and Earthlings expressed their agreement with that statement.

Getting back to the travelers' problems, Thoranthin said, "We would certainly like to help you. We have some rich fertile land to the east of us between our capitol city, Emon and the city of Radin. Your people could set up a colony there if you'd like."

"I'm sure I speak for all of us when I say that we are very appreciative of your generous offer, and we thank you very much," said Queen Virena.

York and Simpson walked outside while the others continued to talk. They ran into Quartin and Lasin.

"I've been wanting to ask if you got home on time after our first meeting," said York.

"No, we didn't," said Quartin, as both boys hung their heads.

"I hope you didn't get into trouble with your father," said Simpson.

"Well, we didn't get completely grounded, but we might as well have been, because Dad restricted us to just eight parsecs from home," lamented Lasin.

And so we close this story of the brave group who finally found a life-supporting planet orbiting an outer star of an outer galaxy, literally at the edge of our universe, ten billion light years from Proxima Centauri.

THE END

ABOUT THE AUTHOR

The Author was born December 4, 1943 in Rapid City, South Dakota. Rapid City lies right at the foot of the beautiful Black Hills of South Dakota.

As a boy Larry just loved clear nights he would look in wonderment at those pin points of light we call stars. And he wondered what is out there is there life out there.

The moon was a very special celestial body to look at it. Because it looked like there were oceans and continents on it's surface. And Larry thought most assuredly that there were moon men sailing their boats on the oceans and seas of the moon. These were the things that inspired Larry.

So the Author then sought out books and magazines on the subject of space and space travel. Larry was also inspired by movies such as *Destination Moon* and *The Forbidden Planet.* And there was *Star Trek* and the moon landings which caused Larry to be in utter awe of it. This made Larry want to travel to the stars in great earnest. But he was to find out that star distances were enormous that it made it prohibitive. But this didn't stop him from dreaming about it. And his Quest to learn more and more about it was never ending.

He later on took a Astronomy course from the South Dakota School of Mines and Technology. This amassed for him a great knowledge. And he also subscribed to Astronomy magazine. And he also belonged to two space organizations the Planetary Society and the National Space Society of which he got a monthly magazine from both.

The Author decided since it was impossible to Physically travel to the stars. The only way to satisfy his desires was to mentally travel the stars. The only way to accomplish this was to write stories of men and women traveling to the stars.

CPSIA information can be obtained
at www.ICGtesting.com
Printed in the USA
FSHW021742291119
64520FS

9 781420 840452